"Hélène Dorion's beautifully poetic novel, *Not Even the Sound of a River*, braids women's stories through various generations. These women are woven into a story that finds its origins in the St. Lawrence River, and that sense of swimming through water, time, and memory is one that is powerful and resonant. Dorion asks readers to consider the value of poetry, art, and a creative life as a way to avoid sinking or suffering when we are faced with the harsh reality of our daily lives. Through grief and loss, poetry and art have 'perhaps begun to save us' during our most challenging trials."
—Kim Fahner, author of *The Donoghue Girl*

"The *Empress of Ireland*'s tragic demise and the lives that have gone with her to the bottom, remain largely unknown. In this richly written book, Hélène Dorion lifts the fog that veiled some of the human stories which the St. Lawrence was only revealing to a few. The book conveys brilliantly the unique allure of this deep river, by exploring the depth of one's personal history."
—David Saint-Pierre, historian and author of *L'Empress of Ireland*

"A gentle tribute to the power of art, and a call to life."
—*La Presse*

"*Not Even the Sound of a River* celebrates the beauty of what has remained mysterious in others, and is revealed one day, as a result of time and chance."
—*Le Devoir*

"A short novel of great beauty."
—*Le Soleil*

NOT EVEN THE SOUND OF A RIVER

HÉLÈNE DORION

translated by
Jonathan Kaplansky

LITERATURE IN TRANSLATION SERIES
BOOK*HUG PRESS 2024

`

FIRST ENGLISH EDITION
First published as *Pas même le bruit d'un fleuve* by Hélène Dorion
Original text © 2020 by Hélène Dorion and Éditions Alto
English translation © 2024 by Jonathan Kaplansky

Library and Archives Canada Cataloguing in Publication

Title: Not even the sound of a river / Hélène Dorion ; translated by Jonathan
Kaplansky.
Other titles: Pas même le bruit d'un fleuve. English
Names: Dorion, Hélène, 1958- author.
Series: Literature in translation series.
Description: Series statement: Literature in translation series | Translation of:
Pas même le bruit
   d'un fleuve. | In English, translated from the French.
Identifiers: Canadiana (print) 20240345517 | Canadiana (ebook) 20240345533
   ISBN 9781771669139 (softcover)
   ISBN 9781771669207 (EPUB)
Subjects: LCGFT: Novels.
Classification: LCC PS8557.O748 P3713 2024 | DDC C843/.54—dc23

The production of this book was made possible through the generous assistance
of the Canada Council for the Arts and the Ontario Arts Council. Book*hug Press
also acknowledges the support of the Government of Canada through the Canada
Book Fund and the Government of Ontario through the Ontario Book Publishing
Tax Credit and the Ontario Book Fund.

Book*hug Press acknowledges that the land on which we operate is the tradi-
tional territory of many nations, including the Mississaugas of the Credit, the
Anishnabeg, the Chippewa, the Haudenosaunee, and the Wendat peoples. We
recognize the enduring presence of many diverse First Nations, Inuit, and Métis
peoples, and are grateful for the opportunity to meet, work, and learn on this
territory.

TRANSLATOR'S PREFACE

I first saw Hélène Dorion speak at a round table at the Blue Metropolis International Literary Festival back in 2003, participating in an event called "Écrire une vie" with Antonio D'Alfonso, Marguerite Paulin, and Noël Audet. Her voice and words captivated me. I wanted to know more about her, and especially to read the book she had just written and discussed at the panel, *Jours de sable*. That evening, I went to Renaud-Bray bookstore and bought a copy. I finished it the next morning, and so much of it resonated with me. In it Hélène Dorion speaks of the summers she spent at Old Orchard Beach in Maine as a child, her love of the ocean, of water, of the grandeur of that scene. I myself grew up by the ocean and spent time in Maine as a child. A couple of days after I read the book, Marc Côté of Cormorant Books asked me if there was a work in particular I wanted to translate. I told him *Jours de sable*.

Now, years later, I have the privilege of translating a second novel by Hélène Dorion, *Pas même le bruit d'un fleuve*. Less autobiographical than the first, it focuses on a tragedy widely ignored in English Canada: the May 1914 sinking of the ocean liner *Empress of Ireland*, heading from Quebec City to Liverpool, struck by a Norwegian collier off the shore of Pointe-au-Père, near Rimouski, Quebec. In Dorion's novel, a three-generational saga, this tragedy remains central to the narrative and pays tribute to the victims of the disaster, in which more than a thousand souls lost their lives. The wrecked ship was not found until 1964. The tragedy is interwoven into the skein of the novel.

Hélène Dorion is widely known as a poet, and this background informs her writing style. In the novel, Hannah, the protagonist, takes a journey back in time to discover her roots: "Now that I've walked on the sand where my mother's life was lost, that I've been able to anchor

7

my history in hers," Hanna says, "I know that I belong to her." Through it all, Dorion alludes to the power of words, the power of poetry to heal:

"How many days do we live?

"Above all, how many days go by without our being numbed by the years, dulled by a series of footsteps without dreams?"

I hope that my translation, *Not Even the Sound of a River*, leads readers to new discoveries.

—*Jonathan Kaplansky*
Montreal, June 2024

How many days will we live?

The question is as blunt as it is incongruous. If we evade it, the years can trickle by without our seeing them. In the end, nothing would remain but hours that have glided by the way the water of a tributary meets the river, meets the sea, leaving no trace of this passage.

I don't think my mother ever asked herself that question. Each day for her seemed to be an exercise in survival. Between the moments I saw her performing household chores, the ones when she appeared joyful with her friends, and the others when she and my father were at war, she would sometimes stop, stare into a void, into another place that swallowed her up. If I tried to speak to her then, I'd come up against her absence. Simone's face would become a stranger's to me. It was no longer my mother who was there, but an unknown. Today still, I cannot claim I know the whole story. But do we ever know the entire truth about our parents?

Kamouraska, 1949

TO LIVE MEANS FOLLOWING THE TRACES OF THE CHILD THAT WE WERE

At this point in the river, no shore appears on the horizon. You could speak of *the sea*. Here, storms conceal the sky, and sometimes even our dreams.

Just as trees with inextricably entangled branches grow while imprisoning other trees, every story cuts a path between life and death. We never entirely make out all the roots and points of wavering that cause it to break. Or else it does not fracture, but comes closer to the stars that illuminate it slightly. We are not very different from the forests scattered with tall trees, which, like heaps of bones, defy the sky but, from one moment to the next, can dislocate.

Our roots run beneath the ground, invisible; it's impossible to unearth them all. We can try to pull one out, hope it will lead us to another that we can extract as well, and so on until we perceive a meaning in this story that we call *our life*.

Simone advances into the icy water without hesitating. She knows there is no sill of rock, you can only enter suddenly; her feet sink into the cold sand, she braves the first waves and advances again, until the water comes up to her hips. Then she dives. Only after a long while does she come to the surface to breathe.

How long does a night last, she wonders, letting herself glide through the dark water. Nothing frightens those who have lost everything. The sea becomes a cage of darkness. But Simone fears neither the cold nor the blackness that will perhaps persist. Soon her hands will touch the algae and the mud, she goes back down and thinks she rediscovers the painting hanging in her family's living room, a painting she looks at so often, persuaded that it, *Dream of Depths*, teaches her to better see and better understand the movements of life she struggles against, shapes that dissolve and immediately recreate new ones—that is how we paint, how we should live, she tells herself, staring into the vast despair that shifts inside her and slowly swallows the entire blue.

Simone likes these moments when she feels her body go numb. Since water does not know time, time ceases to pass. She closes her eyes and automatically synchronizes the movement of her arms with that of her head, which turns right and then left; she breathes the moment her arm goes just above the water and returns to slap against the waves.

She swims, and as long as we swim, she tells herself, we cannot drown. She likes to feel that each sequence distances her thoughts a little more, for you don't think when you're swimming, there are too many worlds—that of tumult and beauty, or the void that grabs at you and the fullness that sustains—too many worlds for thought to be able to interfere.

How long does a night last?

The tide is high, the waves powerful. But Simone doesn't see them, she swims, her legs beating out a regular rhythm, and when a wave appears the minute she opens her mouth to breathe, she effortlessly spits back the salt water tasting of tears, tastes the void that no sea can drown. She swims—

there is no shore to reach, she tells herself, it is good for a while to be free, to no longer struggle against the jostling currents, to flutter arms and legs without thinking, trusting in the wheel of time that keeps on turning, regardless of what happens. Unless that's what living is—entering the current without bypassing the reefs and shallows, without avoiding the stones that the tide will soon hurl upon the shore. The sky is sometimes a consolation; when no black bird scratches the surface, this blue becomes a refuge where the earth describes itself, and

sometimes it seems moved
that we listen to it so well—
when we do, it reveals its life
and then says nothing else.

Simone looks up. Through the mist that ripples above the water, she thinks she notices something, a small boat or perhaps a rock, one of those rocks difficult to detect and that graze the hulls of reckless boats.

Toward what island am I drifting? she wonders. An island where we no longer really exist, where we seek a point of light in the middle of the night, a source toward which we're drawn, a shore that could be a beginning of the world or of our own existence, the nothingness that strikes nothingness and begets millennia, a few atoms in the hollow of nothingness, and that suffices for life to begin.

She closes her eyes, stops moving her arms, as if to see if the water's goodness can carry her. Can she float not knowing where the wind comes from and where the tides are headed?

Lying on her back, arms stretched out to the side, open like light sails on the water's surface, head immersed, Simone now hears only the muffled sound of the world. It is the sound of memories, of torn sails, of broken masts, of too-high waves that crush ships. She begins spontaneously to recite a poem she copied out in a notebook:

Man—a free man—will always love the sea
and its endlessly unrolling surge
will contemplate his soul as in a glass
where gulfs as bitter gape within his mind.

The current carries her to the open sea, or is it clouds flowing in a confused river, a fluid architecture, birds gliding like flotsam in a sky of thunderstorms and ruins.

What do we feel, she wonders, when water goes up our nose, fills our eyes and runs into our stomach, what do we feel when it slides through the entire body and grips us until we choke? At what point do we know it's too late, that we can no longer return? And how to imagine that the sometimes still majestic river can suddenly become a poison in its victims' mouths?

Simone abandons herself to the uncertain landscape, but a stronger wave jostles her. When her body begins to slip into darkness, she arches her back, heaves herself up, and turns onto her back. Eyes open, she looks at the foam-filled sky, tells herself that night will not end, the sound of memories will trouble her for a long time still. This sky holds no promise. Simone no longer feels her arms or legs, she lets herself drift, hoping to wind up on a reef.

Montreal, 2018

GOING BACK HOME (WHERE YOU DESCRIBE YOUR HUNT, YOUR JOURNEY, YOUR HARVEST, YOUR ORIGINS)

I've always hated the smell of chlorine. When I was a child, my parents forced me, all summer long, three times a week, to take swimming lessons that began at seven-thirty in the morning. I'd already be shivering when I arrived at the neighbourhood pool. On those days, I'd wake up feeling nauseous, unable to eat anything before getting on my bicycle, unsteady, terrorized by the idea of having to slip into that water still cold from the night air. I had to learn how to float, swim on my stomach, back, and sides, kick my legs and arms or stretch them out as far as possible and bring them back slowly, controlling my breathing to coordinate it with the movement of my body. In the middle of summer, an entire course was devoted to life-saving techniques. It was the worst morning. For hours, the instructor pretended to drown, and each child in turn had to jump into the water to free her from the stranglehold that, in other circumstances, could truly prove fatal. Later I had nightmares. I saw my mother in the open sea, waving her arms in all directions while I remained motionless on the quay, feet transformed into long roots tied to the wooden planks. Or I was choking under the weight of water closing in above my head. I felt the power of the current sucking me toward the bottom, little air bubbles creating strange shapes as they burst from my mouth, then everything went black.

Each time the smell of chlorine rises to my nostrils, those horrible summer mornings resurface. They bring back images of my body sinking into an abyss until it touches a rough bottom. My eyes are closed, my mouth about to open, my heart begins to beat so loudly that I might not be able to rise back up to the surface and return to the light that appears so far away, I can scarcely make out a shimmer, a shaft of light through which I could pull myself away from the predator.

One day I saw my mother enter the sea as if she were embracing the body of a loved one, as if the violent blows of the waves against her hips were those of a lover to whom she was abandoning herself. For her, the water wasn't glacial, the sun wasn't burning her skin. The wind swept through her hair, revealing her beautiful features and forcing her to plant her feet more firmly in the sand. Was she looking for something at the end of the void, was she waiting for the sea to throw up debris that reappeared on the surface like the sound of memories? My mother then, once again, became a stranger to me. After a while, Simone turned around and returned to the beach, face wet with tears and foam, body exhausted, broken by a strange confrontation with herself.

We probably never fully know the faces nearest to us. They remain enigmas, despite the years we shared with them, intimacy that may never again be recreated. Those present since our birth, those who were there with us for our first steps, our first words, and our first falls as well, remain unfinished mosaics.

At times perhaps we manage to grasp a few fragments that bring a part of the face into focus, modify another. Their faces erase as we approach, then begin to take shape a little more clearly, we hear the murmur of their lives, whose threads and knots they had concealed, obscuring the heavy shadows and keeping doors half closed. We hear the endless swaying from their world to ours, like a tide carrying with it unknown pieces of our own story, the swell of events we did not suspect. And at times, strange faces fill in some of the gaps from which the meaning of that figure, both simple and complex, escaped—a father, a mother who gave birth to us.

The sting of doubt, delving into the heart of things—can I catch the missing piece of a life abandoned like the old shell of a crab that had to moult to continue to grow?

THE WORLD OF CHILDHOOD IS A HANGING GONDOLA WAITING FOR SOMETHING TO ARRIVE

The times my mother remained seated, silent, appearing lost in thought, I did not imagine that she could be suffering. There were so many other times when she spoke, laughed, moved about in every direction to finish one thing or begin another, I could not imagine that, well before I was born, a bomb had burst open inside her. The grief had spread to her heart, her stomach, her head and her gaze, and had never come back out.

One day my mother told me: *If you didn't cry, Hanna, I'd forget to feed you!* At the time I'd found it funny, she must have wanted to let me know how good I was being, but today I don't know. In which house, in which life, was she living then?

Simone forced herself to merely survive, to get through the days by fulfilling her obligations as a mother, her duties as a wife, and by assuming her responsibilities as a daughter and sister. Today I believe that she couldn't wait to reach the end of her journey. But I didn't tell myself that. I couldn't, didn't, want to see it.

So, when she had to face death, she didn't try to postpone it. *Prolonging her life* was out of the question. She had a fit of rage, rebelled slightly, took one last look at the happy moments, the people dear to her, the beauty of the sky in the early morning when she arose before the others to watch the day rise through the window, but nothing could have held her back, not even sadness, to make her delay the time of leaving.

As soon as she met with the doctor, Simone was clear: *Don't do anything to extend my life.* I was with my friend Juliette in the hospital room when my mother uttered those words. I had trouble believing she didn't want to try anything, that nothing and no one could make her want to remain a few months or weeks more, if it were possible.

When she returned home, I suggested we go to Kamouraska, I knew how much she loved the maritime landscape where she'd spent her youth. Of course she didn't speak of it, never referred to the past; for a long time it was my father who filled in the holes in the story—*What did my grandfather do for a living, Adrien, do you remember?*—telling us of summers by the river in the village where their friends were, that's how they met, how they began seeing one another, he and my mother.

Simone seemed to have forgotten so many things about her own life, but perhaps she did not want to remember.

She refused to return to Kamouraska. I had suggested that a nurse come with us to put her mind at ease. I would have rented a large, comfortable car, we would have taken the Route des Navigateurs that runs along the river. Already, crossing the Quebec Bridge, she would have seen Lévis, the city where she'd hated living when Adrien declared bankruptcy and was forced to sell their luxurious apartment in Sainte-Foy. For a privileged woman from Quebec City's Upper Town, living on the south shore was something to be ashamed of, she so resented my father for forcing her to live in a place that was neither city nor suburb, and how she hated the four-room apartment overlooking a parking lot whose lighting ruined every evening. She never invited her friends over during the four years of that exile. I've lost my bearings, she said, I no longer feel at home. But, in reality, she'd never been happy anywhere.

Coupled with the shame of living in Lévis was fear, because now she had to cross the bridge to reach the city, the *real* city, the one where her friends lived, where she liked to take walks and go shopping. But the bridge added to the danger of driving, especially in winter, she was already afraid of so many things—accidents, illness—in fact, she seemed to be on the lookout for any possible fractures of existence, the moment when the dike gives way, when the dam cracks, and the slightest movement in that sense threw her into a stupor whose depths amazed me each time.

My mother did not want to go over her life journey in reverse, the ice could have given way, the fog lifted, she would have lost sight of the horizon and, with it, death.

Today I know it was mainly for me that I wanted to take this journey. To spend a few days alone with her, to join her in her silence, and for her to join me in mine. I wanted to enter my mother's field of vision, for her to enter her daughter's, for us, one last time, to attempt to dwell in that bond, and for the painful sensation to subside that being with her was like being with a stranger.

I so would have liked to drive with my mother, even silently. This silence would have become our words, we would have been together as we never had before, would have watched the names of villages pass by—Cap-Saint-Ignace, L'Islet-sur-Mer, Saint-Jean-Port-Joli, Rivière-Ouelle, and finally Kamouraska, the shore of her youth.

We could have perhaps continued to L'Isle-Verte and Rimouski, before the other shore of the St. Lawrence River, where we'd gone so often when I was little, we'd have rediscovered our memories in Baie-Saint-Paul and Les Escoumins, where one autumn day a cousin of hers invited us aboard his fishing boat to go whale watching in the open waters. My mother remained crouched in a corner of the small boat, and I went to join her. Huddled against her, I pretended to be afraid, it brought us together. She told Adrien she had to stay with me, that I was terribly afraid of the water. It was not entirely false, I'd almost drowned when I was five. We were at the seashore, my parents were distracted, perhaps quarrelling again on the beach, and during that time I almost stopped breathing beneath the wave that had just carried me away. Until a hand lifted me up. My father had run into the water, grabbed me by my cotton sweatshirt that had become too heavy.

My mother had almost no appetite anymore, but I'd have suggested we go to small restaurants along Route 132, and we'd have found a motel along the river. In the mornings, we'd have strolled along the beach, breathing in the smell of kelp and salt water, perhaps she'd have looked out into the distance, and with her I'd have observed the expanse of her life that had become erased the way a horizon disappears after one's looked at it for hours. Perhaps she'd have spoken to me of her childhood and her youth, of those years that presented their possibilities to her, all the paths that suddenly become clear so you don't know which to choose—which landscape to embrace: the sea to learn of storms or the forest to discover the undergrowth.

How many days do we have to see the people who created us through their entire beings, through the entirety of their lives, and not only through an angle that reduces them to being the father, the mother that they were? How long will they have to join us, to look at us the way we expect, that will tell us a bit about what we are and confirm our existence?

Strolling along the river, Simone might have spoken of the time when she became my mother, of when my father died, and I'd have asked her why she never left him, despite the constant tension, the sometimes violent conflicts. Why hadn't she left, with or without me, and what was she thinking of on those nights, motionless at the window, awaiting his return? The absent one, those days tormented by incessant quarrelling, this silent suffering, as vast as a river become an ocean— everything closed again before her.

She hadn't wanted to go down this road of time. No more road, no more horizon. As if she couldn't distance herself from her death. It was no longer the time to go elsewhere. Especially not toward the past. My mother told me: *No*. Explaining nothing, just a *no* closing off the rest.

Eight weeks later, she took away everything, starting with the story that in a sense was my own.

For her it was the end, but for me something was beginning.

THERE IS THIS LIGHT THAT FALLS

A few days after her death, I went to empty what remained in her apartment. A charitable organization had already come to collect the furniture, I had to sort through objects and boxes filled with papers. I needed to hurry because the owner of the residence threatened to charge me rent for the following month if I did not vacate it within a week!

In the middle of the three rooms, I felt as if I were surrounded by remainders of Simone's life, but also by the ruins of my childhood, this landscape that suddenly escaped me.

I began with a box containing about ten elephants, their trunks raised, that Simone liked to collect. I would sometimes bring them back for her from my journeys, they were in a box together with some nautical instruments, including an old compass and a nautical chart of the St. Lawrence from the 1950s that I decided to keep, just for their beauty. I didn't know she liked navigation objects, I'd always thought she hated anything to do with boats.

Then I opened a box filled with all kinds of papers. I sat on the floor in the middle of the living room and picked up a large pile of sheets and postcards, a few envelopes that were addressed to her, and several notebooks.

Simone had kept each of the cards I'd sent her on my travels. What a strange sensation to hold them now in my hands and read what I wrote to her from Spain, Finland, Argentina, or Sweden, brief news of my stays, a few words about the weather, and each time the same question—how are you?—to which no one ever replies.

Photos slipped out of the pile. In one of them, I am in Simone's arms. My father must have taken it, I am maybe two or three years old, there is a cottage behind us and a lake as well. She is smiling, but something in her gaze appears far away, even a little sad. This is the gaze I have never been able to explain to myself.

In another photo, she's in a man's arms and must be about twenty, he looks to be much older, perhaps forty, and they appear close to one another, a kind of intimacy you can sense in their body language, his hand rests on Simone's shoulder, her head is slightly tilted, as if they were touching each other inwardly more than what is outwardly shown in the photo. The man is not her brother, or my father, perhaps he is an uncle I didn't know, or one of her cousins, it must have been a family celebration and Simone was meeting up with a relative she hadn't seen in a long time.

Behind the pile of photos sits one of my childhood note-books, four-coloured with lined or squared pages, in which all students take their notes in class. I imagine it must be one she decided to keep as a souvenir, she who didn't like to hold on to the past.

Opening it, I recognized Simone's handwriting.

Quebec City, 1947

SHE HAD LOVED HIM INTENSELY

The first time she saw him, she felt an irresistible force seize hold of her. He was laughing with his group of friends, they were in the harbour, Simone was strolling with her friend Charlotte and noticed a man taller than the others, more handsome too, and clearly older. The masts were swaying behind him, like a forest trembling. He looked at her as well, while continuing to laugh with his friends. Simone and Charlotte made their way toward the quays, the man did not take his eyes off her, and when the two young women passed in front of the group, he approached.

Simone doesn't know how to answer when he speaks to her, asking if she sails. She'd never boarded a sailboat, had only watched them, fascinated by the grace of the high-masted boats unfurling their sails that carry them out to the open waters. She often goes to the harbour to stroll along the quays, likes seeing the sailors slowly rigging their sailboats, departing the dock, and leaving the city's beauty behind them to reach that of the water. She imagines the view of Cap Diamant from the river, today she asked Charlotte to come strolling with her, *No, I'm not in school*, Simone replied, *I work as a secretary for an insurance company, but excuse me, we have to go now...*

She loved him. Intensely.

That irresistible force had woven its way into her. They saw each other again a few days later. Then another time, and yet another. He showed her the light chiselling the water's surface and let her hear the silence of the stars. With him, she knew the strength of desire and the pleasure of the flesh, slow hours of loving one another, from one tide to the next, their naked bodies lying on the deck, hands intertwined like their entire lives, a strong and complete love unthreatened by anything.

From the moment Antoine embraced her and gently led her to the bed at the back of his sailboat's cabin, from the moment they joined each other naked and looked each other straight in the eye, whisked away by the current, together becoming four arms and four legs intertwined, as soon as they brought their faces together and their mouths met in a kiss that obliterated time, Simone knew she would never stop loving him and would never leave him. From that moment, their impassioned bodies aflame, she knew that her greatest sorrow would be to live without him.

When they left Antoine's sailboat, it was as if their bodies still reeled beneath the strength of their love. Bound together by a slight dizziness, they swayed to and fro as they walked, their embrace prolonged on the never-solid ground that could not interrupt it.

In the street, people looked at them. They were both handsome and very much in love, but as he could have been her father, if they noticed their intimacy, people on the lookout for scandal turned around, muttering, or looked at them disapprovingly. It didn't bother them. Simone didn't have any doubts, she knew Antoine was the love she'd sometimes imagined could exist, a love to which she would give everything. And from that love, she'd receive everything.

She knew that together they would navigate many rivers, go through the worst storms and the slowest deserts, and that the winds, when they came, would end up subsiding.

Montreal, 2018

WE PLANT OUR WORLD SOMEWHERE, ELSEWHERE OR NOT

Juliette left the elevator just as I was about to open my door. In the hallway, I piled a few empty boxes and two others that were still full.

After reading half of one of the notebooks, I know that my mother loved, intensely, and that she suffered, also intensely. Between the two, a void.

Juliette and I have always walked together in those fragile moments, when the road swerves or the winds are too high, our steps are in harmony, our words intersect like our destinies did when we were children.

I was six years old, my mother and I waiting our turn to buy movie tickets. Behind us, a woman was holding her little girl by the hand. She complimented my mother on the coat she was wearing. The line was long, and their conversation lasted some time. Juliette and I both released our mothers' hands to go play together, waiting until it was time for the show. Our house was a few streets away from theirs. Our mothers didn't become friends, but in the years that followed, they would drop us off more and more frequently at one or the other's.

The same school, the same games, the same friends, the same joys, and the same fears, my childhood and Juliette's developed in a similar way. We decided to be *best friends*. The name counted as much as a pact.

At that age, we'd do everything to make these bonds that are difficult to form last, we wanted our *forever friend*, we imagined that our world would collapse if she changed schools or if her family moved.

Juliette did not change schools and her family remained in Quebec City. We remained *best friends forever*, with the flashes of wit necessary to learn that the bonds entrusted to the harshness of existence entail breaches and ups and downs. With the friend, we enter a garden to gather roses, but sometimes you also have to hoe the earth and pull up weeds. The bond will be tested. If we consent to be vulnerable, it will not be exempt from rifts, disappointments, perhaps disillusions; if we consent to be true, it will create doubts and misunderstanding. We want the bond as free as possible, and cultivate and protect it like a rare plant.

Juliette often repeats to me that the absolute I am seeking does not exist. Contradictory beings, that's what we are, she tells me, imprecise creatures, full of contrasts, hanging between joy and sadness, between forever and never, ambiguous beings who have trouble accepting ambiguity. We doubt, and that's what pushes us to explore, to let our gazes drift to welcome along our way what arises, the little wonders that transform us. We are human, and imperfection makes us alive. Your cravings for the absolute will not hold, you will see, one day perhaps you'll no longer need them.

The joyful and turbulent friendships of the little girls we were have transformed into a bond that shared hardships have deepened. A few short-lived but necessary rifts have also kept it anchored in the present, so that it sustains not only memories we don't want to let go of, for fear of losing our childhood along with them, but also what belongs to the flow of days.

On the threshold of our adult lives, we chose similar paths, Juliette went to study visual arts, and I literature. Our buildings neighboured one another, so we spent most of our free time together. She wanted to become a painter, and I a writer, and we each managed to clear the way for the path desired.

The lines of our existences took shape throughout the years like brilliant beams of life making their way through a dense forest.

Today, Juliette is represented by gallery owners in Montreal, New York, and Paris. She has also begun to receive proposals to exhibit in Spain and elsewhere in Europe. While she now lives very well from her work and can devote herself to it entirely, during the first ten or twelve years of her career, she had trouble paying the rent of the tiny apartment we shared. In one corner of the main room, we set up my writing table, and in the other a work bench next to a wall where Juliette hung her work. While places can shift the course of lives, before even the outline of our own is clear, this apartment was the one we had hoped for.

I'll never make it, Juliette would sometimes explode, slamming the front door. I've had it with teaching every evening after ten-hour workdays... Maybe I should give it all up. Then she would go into the bedroom and only come out again hours later. If she were smiling then, I knew it was because she'd spoken to Abby.

She had met Abby Rowan at a conference at the university. A visual artist from New York known for her work as a painter and sculptor, Abby settled in Montreal, where working and living conditions were more favourable. She hired Juliette as an assistant, but also became her mentor.

Juliette liked the work as an assistant. She stretched the

canvases over wooden frames, cleaned paintbrushes, filed and put away works once they were completed. She was also in charge of preparations for exhibitions, including contacts with gallery owners. But even more she liked conversing with Abby, who taught her the foundations of various techniques, possibilities for materials, and especially how matter and shape can become a strong and distinctive expression of the self.

You have the necessary passion to find your own voice, Abby told her. An artist's life is constructed with chaos, and we can only speak of shadow and light calling to one another, of things living and inert, real and imaginary, that match each other. It seems strange to dedicate your life to art, especially in a society that incites performance and entertainment, but that is what gives sense to mine every day. You will face many fears you do not suspect are inside you, you will encounter pitfalls, even more because you're a woman, but when I see you in front of a blank canvas or listen to you speak about the works of some artists, I know you will have no other choice but to go deeper into the path before you.

In Abby's words, Juliette found an antidote to her doubts, and when she went through difficult periods, I too reminded her that her life was that workshop of shapes and colours where her cravings and contradictions came together.

A BREATH OF WATER IN THE DARK

As a child, I hated drawing. It was words that intrigued me. When Juliette took out her coloured pencils, I traced what, without being them, looked like letters. I was eager for them to transform into words before my eyes, then into sentences. The day I came home from school after reading a word for the first time, everything changed. I now had access to another universe, different from the one where words were projected violently onto the walls of the house. Words touched things, making them come alive.

The first time Abby read us a poem out loud, it was like a blade tearing the bank of fog that floated inside me. The shock I'd felt as a child, when a word suddenly appeared, I felt once again. This time, the words gave rise to shadows, gave rise to light, shaking up reality, revealing to me a part of what I had not yet sensed. My sight grew sharper, nothing was ordinary anymore, the world was finally unveiled, it could be expressed otherwise and contained more presences than I had perceived until then.

Since that day, poetry is both my quest and the instrument of my quest. I needed something to gather what had been turned upside down, to name what was torn inside me.

Perhaps I also hoped that books, and later music, to which Abby also introduced us, would tell me where I was from and what I could become. I found in art a call to live, to not make existence just an accumulation of gestures, chores, and objects.

What a contrast when I returned home, alone with my passions, the way my mother was with her silence.

Then I wanted to write, I too wanted to open the window of words so they could reinvent the horizon. That's how this strange undertaking began that, from one book to the next, pushes me to dig in language furrows of hope and of questions.

Abby kept repeating to me to concentrate on writing and not on what ran alongside it. Write, she told me, for yourself to silence the doubt so it doesn't deprive you of the pleasure of creating a world of words that will take root in the real. Don't take your eyes off the path that writing will open. Art is a way of shedding light on the shapes of the world that remain hazy.

So I wrote, prolonging the day when I returned home from school reading everything to be found on my path, amazed that words, those tiny, seemingly inoffensive and worthless instruments, allowed me to dive into the wave of muddled emotions that ran through me.

Juliette and I began presenting our works almost at the same time. One year after the first group exhibition in which she participated, the first novel I wrote was published. It was called *A Sometimes Cloudy Sky*. Through the character of a little girl whose mother is dead, and who held no place in her family severed from its roots, I rid myself of my childhood distress. Persuaded that something had frozen there, I slipped into this novel what I hadn't been able to say to the woman who never embodied that maternal figure for me. I took possession of myself again in another narrative, imagining a story that filled in the flaws in my own into this novel.

I had long questioned my parents to know their past, but only my father answered my questions. Simone remembered nothing, not even her youth.

There was a launch in a bookstore. My mother seemed to feel a strange mixture of pride, worry, and distrust. Perhaps she was afraid we'd discover, in the character of her mother, another face of her.

In the newspapers two things were said that she didn't like: my parents were divorced and my mother had had lovers. One day she telephoned to reproach me for writing that. We never spoke of it again.

Three years later, I published another novel, Juliette had another exhibition, and Abby went to live in Australia, where her work was held in increasingly high esteem. Her departure brought Juliette and me closer together. We remained connected to Abby, who continued to follow our career paths from afar. Juliette now exhibits regularly in Montreal and abroad, I still publish novels, but no one knows that I also write poems, not even Juliette.

They say there is always at least one secret between two people—that is mine with her.

THE RIM OF THE HEART IS CLOUDY

Juliette and I go into the kitchen to make coffee. I talk to her of the notebook I found at my mother's and in which my mother tells her story. The blank page I could not fill was therefore written by Simone.

You never knew that your mother wrote? Juliette asks me. That woman was so secretive, she seemed to float above life—or below it—following winds that she alone could sense. My parents aren't in the least mysterious, that's why Simone fascinated me so. But I know that you always suffered from the distance she kept between you. Like a world that burst into a multitude of fragments, you were two continents that kept drifting far from one another, land that wandered and transformed itself as it went along. With her death, perhaps something is coming together inside you?

I don't know. I spent my life with words. All these years, they taught me to better read the world and people, to discover meaning and create it. Today I find myself again before my mother's story as if before a foreign language.

And what if I didn't manage to reconstruct these fragments so they fit into my own story? What if, rather than shedding light on my footsteps, these notebooks uprooted me from what I know of myself and transformed what I believe I know about Simone?

THE SHADOWS HAD ALREADY FALLEN

Can poems save us from sinking? Can they blow on the fog that erased the horizon and unveil those mountains we had not yet seen, whose existence we hadn't even suspected?

In the box where the notebook and the mariner's compass were found, there was also a newspaper clipping.

Beneath the photograph of a ship, a journalist describes his shock at seeing hundreds of corpses aligned in the shed of the Rimouski wharf. In that improvised morgue, people tried as best they could to identify the bodies arriving, similar in the anonymity of their creased skin and their swollen faces.

On damp bits of paper, some collected signs that could make it possible to identify the remains, they searched the clothing to recover an object that remained wedged at the bottom of a pants pocket, an embroidered handkerchief, a brooch, a hairpin, or a bottle of tablets—anything that could have brought back a name to one of these corpses.

They had been removed from the water like a school of fish, then set out like slabs of flesh, logs now floating on an anonymous earth, confined to the silence they endured before dying.

The survivors gathered near the drowned. They had managed to extract themselves from the metal carcass that the river engulfed and wash up on shore. They were asked to give their names and those of their families, who would be informed of the good news. Stammering, they offered their identities, uncertain of still being alive and entitled to utter that name. Those washed up looked in stupor at the drowned who piled up along the walls, forming rows of disarticulated bodies that had to be stepped over to reach the infirmary set up in a corner of the shed.

The next day it would be written:

In death, the rich sleep beside the poor, the powerful beside the weak, the humble Pole or Russian who yesterday was starving in the streets of a Canadian metropolis sleeps beside the golden patrician. Now they are all equal.

The article, entitled "Horrible Maritime Catastrophe," tells of the event that took place the day before.

Le Progrès du Golfe
Rimouski
Friday, May 29, 1914

The *Empress of Ireland*, colliding with a Norwegian collier, the *Storstad*, at about 1:45 a.m. sank completely within ten minutes, dragging a thousand human souls into the abyss.

Approximately 350 persons to date have been recovered and transported to Rimouski. Of those, many are horribly mutilated and dying.

The *Lady Evelyn* and the *Eureka*, after taking the survivors of the terrible shipwreck to Rimouski, returned to the scene of the tragedy to recover a multitude of hideously disfigured and half naked corpses. The *Lady Evelyn* returned at around 2:00 p.m. with close to 200 drowned on board.

I wanted to know more about it. So I did some research on this accident that, to date, remains one of the largest catastrophes in maritime history. I was hoping to understand why Simone was interested in it.

Rare are the ships that, back then, ventured onto the St. Lawrence in the spring, as there were so many sandbars. Given the shallow depth and narrowness of certain channels, as well as the reefs, thick fog, diagonal currents, it is difficult to avoid all the perils when navigating the river. I found other articles that attempted to explain how the collision could have happened and described the appalling chaos that followed.

It is in May that the *Empress of Ireland*, a luxury ocean liner launched in 1906, reputed to be one of the safest of its time, and that sails between Quebec City and Liverpool, left the port of Quebec at end of day. It stopped in Pointe-au-Père, near Rimouski, to let off the pilot who had guided it from Quebec City, as was the rule. After also unloading a few bags of mail, the ship lifts anchor. Banks of fog begin floating above the waters like unpredictable ghosts. About thirty minutes later, a lookout informs the captain of a ship that is going upriver, twelve kilometres away. The *Empress of Ireland* sends signals and adjusts its course based on that of the other boat.

The night is cold and a thick fog overtakes the river. Around two o'clock in the morning, the ocean liner is struck. The Norwegian collier the *Storstad* has just rammed into its right side, immediately creating a large opening. In a few seconds, tens of thousands of gallons of water penetrate the hull of the *Empress*, which launches an SOS, and fourteen minutes later, the ocean liner stops heeling over and sinks in the peaceful waters of the river, scarcely visible to the passengers who rushed to the deck. Some dive in, while others fight over the few dinghies that can be lowered. Soon the ocean liner is completely engulfed.

A little more than an hour after the distress call launched by the *Empress*, rescue arrives aboard two ships, the *Eureka* and the *Lady Evelyn*, which recover 465 survivors. The crew of the *Storstad* also takes part in the life-saving operations.

That night, 1,012 people perished. It is said that most of those who died were third-class passengers, whose cabins were located on the lower decks. Of the 138 children aboard the *Empress of Ireland*, only five survived.

The wreck of the *Empress of Ireland* lies at the bottom of the river, about eight kilometres from the village of Sainte-Luce-sur-Mer. It was only found in 1964, exactly fifty years after the catastrophe, by a group of amateur divers. At a depth of forty-three metres, they suddenly saw an immense mass emerge among the thin rays of light pointing toward the carcass listing heavily to the right. At the time, they ignored the weight of their discovery; it was only after they returned to the surface that they thought of the *Empress of Ireland*.

What do the divers find with this corpse of rust sunk into the sand that confines ageless bodies, names that the sound of a river suffocated? How many other lives did just one of the faces imprisoned in the dark and cold destroy—mouth open, a cry never voiced—the burden of a human history? And, side by side, soon the unnamed join the survivors washed up on the ground that is imposed upon them like a stele forever uncompleted, a light boat pierced more and more with each passing each year. Others still remain captive of that night, and their name becomes a worn secret, covered by the algae and nibbled at by shellfish. But neither the waves nor the years will fill an absence noisier than the lives.

The affair was closed following two parallel investigations whose conclusions contradicted one another. One described a change of course ordered when nothing at all could be seen, the other blamed an officer who delayed too long in calling his captain. It is reasonable to believe that navigation errors could have been made on both sides, that the fog signals and audible alarms were difficult to clearly interpret in these dangerous conditions. Further investigations were abandoned like the shipwreck.

Hanna unfolds the page of the yellowed newspaper. She doesn't know what she's looking for among the old papers that emit a strong odour of dampness. Her mother must have had a reason for keeping them, but no more than her grandmother Eva, Simone had never spoken to her of this sinking. Hanna must dig deeper to know why her mother felt connected to this event that mainly concerned the families of immigrants come to settle in Canada at the beginning of the century.

The day after the tragedy, while research continued around the still-visible shipwreck, among the debris wandering at the water's surface, while boats returned from the river filled with the drowned, a list of survivors was published, the names of those who washed up returning to us as if from the depths of the waters. Never would they cease to feel, upon the back of their necks, the silence of the dead.

James Wilson · Art Carmichael · Elatha Carmichael
· David Carmichael · Dagan Ross · Cormac Skinner
· Brenda Skinner · Etan Cunningham · Fiona
Cunningham · Mary Cunningham · Mark Williamson
· Neal O'Neil · Tara O'Neil · Kate O'Neil · Glenn
Monaghan · Ula Monaghan · Lucharba Baron · Peter
Baron · Ann Baron · Shanleigh Cowan · Tomas Cowan
· Trevor McCormack · Kiara McCormack · Iosep
McCormack · Iollan McKinney · Alisson McKinney ·
Dillon O'Sullivan · Dallan O'Sullivan · Braden Bannon
· Thomas Hogart · Dorothy Hogart · David Ferguson ·
Robert Robinson · Claire Robinson · Mark O'Connell
· Robert O'Connell · Paul Brennan · Norman Murphy
· Jeff Gilmore · Henry Murray · Caroll Murray · Paul
McCarthy · Lilly McCarthy · Craig Allen · Peter Allen ·
Wallace Ferguson · Gladys Ferguson · Luchar Jordan
· Roan Greenfield · James Gardner · Abbie Gardner ·
Dave Tonner · Berach Tonner · Mark O'Brian · Kara
O'Brian · Nolan McCarthy · Eireen McCarthy · Tomas
McAllee · Aslinn McAllee · Arthur Kelly · Eva Kelly ·
Dylan O'Brien · Branden Baker · Kate Baker · Larry
McAteer · Kelan McAteer · David McAteer · Ailis
Ferguson · Mary Ferguson · Paul Gilbert · Alexander
Quinn · Amanda Quinn · Craig Shannon · Caroll
Shannon · Covey McGivern · Catherine McGivern ·
Fergus Tormey · Doreen Tormey · Ernest Tonner

Route 132 toward Kamouraska, 2018

NOTHING CAN BE UNDERSTOOD WITHOUT INTERLACING

So I took to the road.

I followed the river up to Kamouraska. Simone spent her youth there, I had never yet been. There I met the face of this woman, my mother, about whom I perhaps ignored the essential. At the very least, what I knew of her face blurred as I approached it.

On the road, I imagined Simone by my side, as in the trip we didn't take. I heard her laugh, saw her contemplate the scenery, then turn to tell me some memories of her youth, of that time before the sadness, that time before my father.

From Montreal, I drove for a little more than two hours before arriving in Quebec City. I hesitated to enter the city and see again the houses where we'd lived, I decided to do it instead on the way back. I followed the directions to the 132 that runs along the river, and about three hours later I was in Kamouraska.

Worn out by the journey, I walked into the first inn I came across, Le Manoir de la Mer, and rented a room for the night. Quickly I unpacked my bags to go down to the beach and gaze at the sunset. I sat down on a rock.

Simone by my side, we watch the horizon melt slowly between the memory of happiness and the hope of a possible future. As the absent do, my mother tells me about the hours that shifted far in the past and those that approach like dark waves. Speaking to me in a low voice, she too seems to be seeking something else in this hazy space between the sky and the sea, as if others absent had left a trace.

Is night that moment when nothing moves, the bottom of an ocean whose movement remains invisible to us?

How long does night last? And one day do we know how to go through the hours when we can no longer advance, when we remain motionless, waiting for light to return?

Quebec City, 1948

THE HALF-FINISHED HEAVEN

Antoine watches Le Majestueux—The Majestic—that's what they call the river, at this level, when it meets the sea and its shores are no longer visible. In the waves and foam, he recalls the stories it knows.

I was not born, he says to Simone, who is shivering and comes to snuggle up against him, when the first ships sailed up the St. Lawrence. My father told me this dream he carried; like thousands of other immigrants, he wanted to reach the promised land. Huge steamships were arriving from Europe, from Liverpool and London. They moored at the port of Quebec. People were eager to set foot on this new soil, but when they arrived, instead they were isolated in quarantine at Grosse-Île, a lost island in the middle of the St. Lawrence, to avoid the transmission of cholera, smallpox, and the Spanish flu, all those diseases that decimated entire populations on the other side of the ocean. *Alice*, a steamship, took them there, it went back and forth between the city and the island, but some, already ill during the crossing, never reached the promised land. Anonymous, they wound up on an unknown island, a few steps from a dream they would never attain.

All the beauty of the river... Imagine, my love, he said again to Simone, how many immigrants must have been filled with wonder seeing the small villages that ran alongside it, discovering the churches, lighthouses, and windmills that guided the gaze of sailors, becoming their beacons. At the time, we didn't know all the pitfalls that made navigation perilous. When I look at the river, I see the scene where happy moments unfolded, but also where misfortunes took place. It is our history that circulates through this passageway, it transported what your ancestors needed to survive. My father was proud to take part in it. Along the river we find once more the path of generations who came to start their lives over on this new land that for them was your country. Along the river, we recreate the journey of love and of the conquest, we see the good and evil in the depths of these same cloudy waters of time.

Simone had never felt him so passionate. His voice carried an enthusiasm she didn't know in him.

Antoine let only very few things filter through about his origins. His father, Arthur Corrigan, and his mother, Emma, née O'Hagan, both Irish, died when he was a child, he said without adding details. His real first name was Anthony, but, arriving in Quebec City, his adoptive parents, Jules and Jeanne, decided to Gallicize it. Anthony is *he who feeds on flowers*, taught Simone, for whom the meaning of first names was very important. She based herself on what her own evoked—*she who is fulfilled*—to imagine his future. She had already planned that later, should they have a son, he would be named Adam and begin *a new line*, and should they have a daughter, she would be named Hanna and carry *the grace of life*.

The rare times when Antoine recalled his family, he did it with reserve, as if he were going to betray a secret, or as if the past were so heavy it could not be set down on the fragile present. Simone nevertheless learned that Antoine's parents were born in 1890, and that he was only four when they'd both lost their lives, apparently in a very serious accident. He was then placed in an orphanage in Quebec City and, a few years later, adopted by a childless couple. He didn't say any more about his childhood, except to tell that after being very frightened of the water as a small boy, he had begun to tame his fear. Jeanne and Jules brought him to the shores of the river, beneath the Quebec Bridge, they bought him a miniature sailboat that he'd float a few metres from him, holding it by a string. He learned to manoeuvre it in such a way that he could prevent it from capsizing when the waves rose.

Simone liked Antoine's way of extricating himself from contingencies. To her eyes, he was a man without ties, without a burden, whereas she carried hers so heavily. With him she felt like those boats that unfurl their sails when the wind blows. She had finally gotten rid of her alcohol-ravaged father who made her so ashamed in the busiest bars of Quebec City. When her mother asks her to fetch him to avoid his landing in prison for committing some wrongdoing, she strides through the night hoping to meet no one. She walks in the humiliation of going once again to track down that unbearable father surrounded by women charmed by his lies. Once they leave the bar, she will lead his too-heavy body to a woman who no longer awaited it.

How many times had Simone told her mother to leave that drunkard who was nothing like a father or a husband, but she stubbornly refuses, fearing that being separated or divorced would be a worse shame for her and her children.

Simone could not take a step without this shame weighing on her. She wanted to save her family from what was carrying her away like a blanket of fog.

She turned toward Antoine and thought she saw new land on the horizon. The river is a history of shipwrecks and new beginnings.

When I sail on my boat, Antoine continued, the river becomes a body that goes through seasons—high waves for spring, warm winds of summer, sheets of ice in winter hitting one another, and then the jolts of autumn returning us to the months of bareness when the flow becomes still. All that time, the fish, shellfish, whales and sperm whales, seals and sea urchins tell of a life that the surface of things barely knows.

Les Éboulements, 1949

AT THE END OF THE SUFFERING
THERE WAS A DOOR

Antoine had lifted anchor early in the morning. The day before, he'd prepared his boat, checked the mast, ropes, and rigging, spread the sails to make sure they had no gaps, even tiny, that could be fatal, for while he knew perfectly the currents and obstacles to avoid, he realized that the slightest neglect is unforgiving. He also scrubbed down the deck, oiled the wood that had suffered from winter storage.

He lifted anchor and, immediately upon leaving port, began unfurling the mainsail. The cold was biting, May is still winter on the river, and while the ice had been swallowed up by the sun, the echo of its presence blew on the choppy waters.

How he loved his sailboat! Thanks to Jules's insistence, Antoine ended up conquering his fear of the sea, to the point where he later sailed with friends and decided to acquire a sailboat of his own, used certainly but in perfect condition. He had worked at the port since his teenage years and knew how to recognize a good boat.

The day Antoine officially bought *Beata*—that was how he christened it, evoking the woman beloved by Dante, whose *Divine Comedy* he reread each year—he invited his parents to come see her, and together they remembered the moments when, as a child, Antoine played with the fragile little ship his father had given him.

With Antoine at the tiller that day, the sailboat heads toward the Lower St. Lawrence. It passes Cap-Saint-Ignace, L'Islet-sur-Mer, and Saint-Jean-Port-Joli, the winds are light, night gradually creeps over the horizon, the river barely quivers, as if beginning to doze. On deck, Antoine watches the sky, and this enclosure of solitude from now on will be his home, soon he'll sleep with the waves knocking against the hull like the memory of the past. Does the heart feel beauty at the same time as the eyes see it? He thinks of Simone and tells himself that if one day we understand we have only one life, sometimes we know we will experience only one love.

Antoine goes down into the hold while the river edges its way amid the fog that's beginning to ripple above the cold waters of spring. He takes the book still open on the table, that *Divine Comedy* that he tells himself he'll never be done with. He has crossed the circles of *Hell*, then joined the mountain of *Purgatory*, now he penetrates the mists of the soul that atones for its sins before being able to access the spheres of *Paradise*.

It is difficult to say what happened afterwards. The rain began to fall, dense fog obliterated the river and swallowed up the horizon. Everything became still. It was like being in a painting, a scene the artist set in fluid shapes and washed-out colours. We don't know if the image moved inside, where a motion can be sensed without ever seeing it.

A furious noise broke the silence. Something rammed into the sailboat.

We can imagine that it then lay down on its side like a wounded animal, that the violent collision dug an enormous hole at the water's surface.

Absorbed in his reading of *Purgatory*, Antoine saw nothing of the underground passage the sea had opened.

Under the impact, he was projected against the bulkhead. We may think he hit his head and fell heavily to the ground.

Unconscious, he does not feel the water penetrate the crack that enlarges rapidly, the water gushing forth inside the cabin like black ink, and soon his body begins to float almost lightly as torrents continue filling the hold.

Antoine doesn't hear the shouting outside, doesn't hear the voices that pierced the night like stars—Simone's voice, does he hear Simone's voice just when he wonders if the heart perceives death when it approaches, does the heart know the minutes, the seconds that remain before it fades away like a star?

Can poems save us from sinking, Antoine wonders, repeating to himself these verses of Dante that perhaps open to him the door of *Paradise*?

> *From that most holy wave I now returned*
> *remade, as new trees are*
> *renewed when they bring forth new boughs, I was*
> *pure and prepared to climb unto the stars.*

And the waters, like the poem, close over the sailboat.

Kamouraska, 2018

WE NEVER COMPLETELY LEARN TO BE OUT OF OUR DEPTH

Entering the church, I thought that it was there, perhaps, that the funeral had taken place.

Simone is sitting in the first row reserved for family and close friends, her face scarcely shows the shadow hovering over her. By her side, her mother doesn't take her eyes off the closed coffin. Her thoughts shift back to 1916. Eva sees again the funeral of her fiancé who'd gone to join the front on a grey November day. A few letters later, she would sense his death but was never able to see the inanimate body of this man she was supposed to marry when he returned, yes, they would marry, have children, her life would be happy and leave behind her a peaceful trail.

But he never returned, and she will agree to marry Édouard, an alcoholic who will force her to satisfy his desires, including giving him four children she'll raise alone, while keeping within the face of the soldier who never returned from that war that consumed her future, never would she forget him, not in her dreams nor in the harsh reality of an existence made up of solitude and compromise.

Simone cries in silence, sitting on the wooden bench of the first row of the dark church at the end of this month of May, as if the winter had lasted and would last an eternity, there would be no spring. It is a day of high winds, almost warm, but they chase away none of the emptiness that crashed down upon her, they do not drive away the weight of sadness that each minute steals into her flesh.

The coffin is also empty. There is nothing inside, packages of fabric perhaps, to give the illusion of weight. Antoine's body was not found, it is wandering somewhere at the bottom of the river, eyes closed, arms stretched out sideways probably, strips of flesh already buried by silt. Nibbled at by fish and shellfish, Antoine's body is no more here than is Simone's heart, they lie in the icy waters of death.

For six days, she was away. Did the telephone ring that evening? Did she go to the apartment Antoine shares with a friend, the following morning, after waiting for a sign from him all night, clinging to doubt, did she go to his place, wishing to see the face of the man she loves appear, still unaware that her life, a few seconds later, would never be the same? And was Jules there when the police knocked on the door to inform them of the accident? Did he go to the station to attest to the death of this boy so beloved he'd chosen for a son, hoping to save him from suffering and solitude, this son died in a night of fog from which no one would emerge, neither Simone nor his father, who had allowed Antoine to leave alone with *Beata*? Did he describe the scene of a sailboat leaving the sunny port of Quebec City on that day in May 1949, to travel up the river, but whose trail was brutally erased between Pointe-au-Pic and Kamouraska?

That morning, no one wondered whether poems save us from suffering.

Leaving the church, Simone sees the river. Antoine's coffin is not uninhabited. His body rests like a wreck in this long grave without sides that spits up its dead when it wants, when it can no longer carry the memory.

Simone scans the expanse. The body of my beloved is there, she tells herself. It drifts with the currents, follows the tides, criss-crosses the bottom, brushes up against the algae, bumps against a rock, then comes back up to the surface. One day I'll swim, eyes closed, I'll see a body approach that the river extracted from the earth, I'll grab a hand and recognize it immediately, it will no longer be the river's cold water that embraces me but the arms of Antoine. Soon I'll move toward the waves, his powerful thighs will knock against mine, I'll swim farther still toward the open sea, floating on my back, my head will strike his chest. I'll touch his face one last time, place my lips on his, and our bodies will embrace to never again separate. These are not anonymous ashes that will be given back to me, but the very flesh of our love.

Kamouraska, 1949

I LEFT TO DIVE INTO THE BLACK HOLE OF LIVING

When Simone emerges from the water and returns to the beach, it's the hour she waits for each day. The hour when she'll open a bottle into which her despair can slide. Already the first sip, carrying hope, will begin to lighten the burden, she'll feel the grief dissolve in the fragrance of the alcohol that plunges into the depths of the sea and brings back pipe dreams and numb dragons. The bottle half-empty, there is no more anger, no more sadness, no more diabolic nights clinging to her, nor even any more memories.

Do poems save us from suffering? What use are they when we cross a raging ocean? Are words like shadows that shift at the bottom of caves, and that we end up confusing with what is real?

Simone pours herself a glass and sits down at the table. She opens her notebook. Her mother is upstairs, probably sewing, her sister has not returned from Quebec City, last night there was a big celebration with friends—come with me, she told her, it will do you good, but Simone replied *no*.

In her notebook, she describes meeting Antoine, the story of this love whose irresistible force she continues to feel, even if he is no longer there to pass it on to her. She writes what absence makes more heartrending each day, perhaps the words will alleviate the intensity of the loss, time will do its work, as we say, expanding reality to place the wound at a distance.

Will she be able to allow enough hours, days, and months to enter her heart and her belly for the pain to diminish? She goes round in circles in the passing time. Fortunately there is the wine and also the poems she wrote without knowing where they'd lead her.

I advance amid the tall grasses of absence
without horizon, you, my life
on what shore of love
or of the loss of love
have you washed up?

You have no more story.

Quebec City, 1952

AND I SAW THE CLOSE OF DAY
AND THE FALLING TREE

At the foot of the altar, as she takes her marriage vows, Simone doesn't know what awaits.

Faintly, she repeats after the priest *for better*, but she knows that better can only be love, she repeats *for worse*, and knows that worse is stirring in her body, flowing in each of her veins, her heart an autumn leaf that the winds have already shaken too much. She tells herself that her life will be a chain of days spent between laundry and errands, between school and the grazed knees of children, minor illnesses to treat, the husband who demands, the brother who fails, like his father, a desert she will go through without seeking a source, without even feeling thirst.

Now that she has left her well-paid job as a secretary, her material well-being depends on this man who said he wanted to rescue her from what absence constructs in her.

Simone doesn't know what her life would have been.

But what good is a promise that death can interrupt at any moment, and what is it like, this *worse* that you promise to go through side by side? What weight do such words carry when we know that a kind of fate can take us away from the home we lived in, from the body we embraced every evening and every morning, and that would perhaps come to tear us brutally apart?

Simone and Adrien walk down the aisle. They are *husband and wife*, they kissed in front of their families and friends to validate this union to which no one is opposed, not even Eva, who knows that her daughter is now entering a mutilated existence. But would solitude be any less suffocating, she wonders, hearing the priest seal Simone's fate as hers was one day in 1922? She was twenty-four and Édouard twenty-five, she too had said *yes* before the priest and before her family. She had known him scarcely a few months, he was a kind and good man who worked at his father's print shop in Quebec City. With him, she would be secure. Above all, Eva could no longer await the return of the man gone to the front who was her love and was supposed to be her life. That day, she said *yes*. And the other days, she murmured *no*, clinging to the return of the soldier.

One autumn evening, Adrien invited Simone to the movies. Another evening, to a restaurant. And on those days, contrary to the others, she said *yes*. Among their group of friends, Adrien was no doubt the most charming and the most athletic. He had begun studying architecture in Montreal but had to stop when his father asked him to return to Quebec City to work with him in his plumbing business, almost bankrupt. Of modest origins, Adrien's family lived in the distant suburb of Charlesbourg. Practically the countryside, because all it contained was a few small businesses and houses that had nothing in common with those of the well-to-do neighbourhoods of the Upper Town where Simone's family lives.

For a long time, Adrien was secretly in love with her. More than one obstacle separated them, first of all the way she saw him, just one friend among others.

When he saw Simone broken, sliding into alcohol and

hiding away in solitude, Adrien thought the biggest obstacle was now removed and he should allow time to dilute the sorrow of absence, dissolving what it could not prevent, erasing it like fog gripping the horizon. But Adrien didn't know that suffering is an opaque curtain that separates people from the world. And that while time may lick the tip of the blade, it can never remove it from the flesh.

Even though Simone refused all his invitations, he was not discouraged. One day she said *yes*. They kept company for a few months, then Adrien asked her to marry him. Again she said *yes*.

She doesn't know what her life would have been like.

Perhaps the same, but with, in addition, this irresistible force she so lacks when the time comes to say *yes, I do*, to utter these words like a betrayal of the man whose breath she still feels beating down on her neck; each night, she hears his step and his voice that murmurs love—is it only a dream, she wonders, will I enter a history that will never be mine?

Simone looks at her mother seated in the first row of the church. Didn't Eva *begin anew* and find some happiness with her children? Her marriage collapsed, she placed this husband in the hands of her daughter Simone, who knew how to approach him gently when he was leaning on the bar seducing a woman, a glass in hand. He would have said anything for the woman to meet up with him in one of the rooms of the fashionable Hôtel Clarendon, and people now knew Édouard well, the porter greeted him by name when he arrived, early in the evening. Later, he saw a girl enter who went directly to the bar and approached Édouard, gently placing her hand on his arm to get his attention. As soon as he saw his daughter's face, he gave in. Nodding, he arose immediately like a kid who's been caught, leaving with her and bidding goodbye to the porter who said to him: *See you tomorrow, Monsieur Édouard!*

Has Eva forgotten everything of that loveless marriage that fell apart, whereas today she seems delighted and relieved to see Simone at the foot of the altar with Adrien?

Even if he isn't from our background, Eva tells herself, at least she won't be alone like her sister, two *old maids* in the same family would be too much. Adrien will want to make her happy—isn't that the meaning of his first name, *he who watches over the happiness of his home*?—but my daughter will remain entrenched in the solitude of memory, she also thinks.

Simone doesn't know what her life would have been. Perhaps the same, perhaps that of all women who abandon their studies, or the jobs they have as young people to get married, live in a house that belongs to their husband, do the shopping, the meals, the dishes, have children, give them a bath, put them to bed, and the next day get them out of bed so that they go to school, and all the love in the world suddenly rests on these little beings, all amends are made through them.

Hours that return over and over with their choreographed chores, that is what my life will be, Simone tells herself, a story like that of those women who place other destinies on hold to marry that of their husband. For all that makes sense only if you choose that life, and the line on which we hang out the clothes of the man and the children connects us, rather than being stretched over an abyss we never finish crossing.

Did Simone have the time to dream of a career before Antoine carried away with him the very idea of a dream and accomplishment? Of course this perfectly ordered existence will give her a few breaks—Adrien promises her a good life, on Saturday evenings they'll go as a family to a restaurant, there will be skiing in winter and golf in summer, for one or two weeks, her husband will rent a house by the sea, she'll be able to read on the beach, perhaps even write when the others are in bed. Then she'll feel Antoine's breath on her neck, and in the morning, walking on the sand, watch the warm sea waters that won't swallow up any love.

I must move forward, Simone thinks. I don't know if I'm getting my life wrong by marrying Adrien. But if I don't, what will I become? A single woman at twenty-five, I'll be called an *old maid*, like they call my sister Agathe, unaware that she's seeing a married man in secret, I'll add to the family's dishonour. I can't do that to our mother, who already has the weight of four children and a husband in name only. With no promotion possible, I'll remain a secretary, enduring the contempt of my colleagues, or I'll become the mistress of one of them, dependent on the time and favours he'll bestow upon me. My friends who have already married will soon have children, what use will they have for a single woman at the end of the table on New Year's or at birthdays? Am I being thrown into a life that isn't mine and that will constantly remind me of the extent of my loss?

You are now husband and wife.

LIKE THE CLOUD CHOOSES THE LANDSCAPE

Adrien would have liked things to have gone differently. But he knows that life is a movement we can neither predict nor stop. He also knows that everything transforms, often without our knowing, we don't pay attention to a situation or a person, and when we return, it's not entirely the same face, things have changed. A bit of shade or a bit of light opened one path, closed another.

Adrien did not take his eyes off Simone. His gaze followed her as she walked up the church aisle on the arm of her father, this man who makes an entire family suffer, he tells himself, at least he didn't show up drunk, I don't dare imagine if Simone had to get him out of the Clarendon in the early hours of the morning, and the shame if he'd come in staggering.

Simone smiles while he, Adrien, a plumber's son, watches her. In under an hour, he'll be the husband of this woman with whom he's been in love for years. He observed her constantly, without her noticing, he liked her laughter and her oh so blue eyes, her hair like flames in the wind, this woman will never be mine, he'd thought when he'd learned she was engaged to a sailor older than her.

But how could Simone's mother have let her go out with this man who seemed so unstable and had no real profession, Adrien wonders, as his future wife stops before him, removes her arm from her father's and places her hand in his. At last she'll be my wife and each day with her will be a blessing. May my suffering at seeing them embrace disappear, embracing in full view on the street. Simone seems fulfilled right now, it's as if her eyes are sparkling like I've never seen them sparkle. They all doubt I'll make her happy, but I'll have a good job, we'll live with our children in a big house, so yes, she'll be happy, we'll go to the ocean in summer, to the mountains in winter, our children will have children, and we'll go on treasure hunts on Easter, have magical Christmases, yes, my wife will be happy...

In the pew in the first row, his father, Henri, his mother, Édith, their pride evident, in less than an hour, their eldest son will be married to a girl from the bourgeoisie. Buying new clothes was a good idea, that way we look like we come from the Upper Town, oh she is beautiful, this woman he's marrying, my son will be the best match for her, Henri tells himself, placing his hand on that of Édith, who has tears in her eyes noticing the smile lighting up her son's face—I'd never have thought he'd convince her to marry him, she thinks, I only hope he won't be disappointed, that this woman is aware of what she is doing, marrying one man when you've loved another, I don't know how she manages to smile like that, perhaps she didn't love him as much as was rumoured, it was a bit strange to see them, now they're a real couple, oh my son, as long as he doesn't suffer...

You are now husband and wife.

Kamouraska, 2018

NIGHT HAD TIME TO FALL

Juliette came to join me. I called her two days after I arrived here, and as soon as she heard my voice, she told me she'd take the bus the following morning.

She arrived in the late afternoon. I'd been out walking all day in the village, my mother had also walked on the cold sand, gathered shells that remained intact and stones smoothed over by the sea, like me she walked on the wharf, sat at the very end, legs dangling, and the wind had created clouds in our eyes.

I brought two of the boxes filled with photos, notebooks, and newspaper clippings. Now I know, it's not an uncle or a cousin in the photo, it's him, Antoine, not quite young anymore, beside my mother who must be barely twenty and seems so happy. It may be the only photo she had of him, the sole proof of their love.

Sometimes perhaps she would open the drawer of her night table and cast her gaze into Antoine's to regain that strength she must miss, in the evenings, when she slid beneath the covers and joined her husband, turning her back to him—did she miss this strength in the morning when she prepared breakfast for my father and me, and on Christmas Eves, coming out of Mass, heart swaying, did she believe in the resurrection of souls and remission of sins, did she think that in the end there remains of us but dust of ashes made up of creased flesh, listless organs, and a few bones gnawed by the earth? Did she understand that you can be taken to the depths of a sea that exerts such cruelty that any idea of faith in something invisible or immaterial is immediately dismissed?

Simone had several faces. The first, sad and gloomy, that of seaside and twilight; the second, angry, that of household drudgery and material existence; the third, radiant, aperitifs and evenings with plenty of wine between friends, and with her friend Charlotte or her sister Agathe, when she let herself be taken far from her reality—Malaga, Granada, Lisbon, Faro—she returned from them with strength, giggling, her heart brightened.

As a child, when we left on vacation, I rediscovered my fear of the ocean. I dreaded the moment my father would take me by the hand so we could swim together, the waves seemed so high and so rough, but I didn't let my fear show, I smiled, wondering why my mother never came with us. She would remain on the shore, staring fixedly until she opened a book or a notebook and began to write. I'd forgotten that memory, but I see her again now, placing her beach bag filled with all her worries and precautions on her knees, telling my father and me to go ahead and walk without her, and when we return, she quickly closes the notebook.

When Juliette arrived, we went to eat in the restaurant I'd found the day before, overlooking the river.

Throughout the journey to come and meet you, Juliette said to me, I thought about what you told me. I understand why you're shaken up. Clearing, digging, sifting, and raking is always a way of laying yourself open to beginning anew.

When I paint a canvas, Juliette continues, I first arrange the colours with large brush strokes. Then I let the surface dry slightly before coming back to it and smooth it with a metallic instrument I made myself. I let the paint harden a bit again. Each stage of drying and smoothing shifts the painting, frees it from what it was, bringing it to what it may become, adding a new story to those it carries. In this way I retouch the surface until all the pentimenti fade and transform into a new beginning that calls forth a new painting.

Midway through the evening, we returned to the hotel, and with Juliette I opened the boxes that would bring the bond that until then I'd shared with my mother somewhere else.

THERE WAS A LITTLE MORE LIGHT IN THE WATER

We spread out the newspaper articles on one of the two beds in the room. They all concerned the sinking of the *Empress of Ireland*.

Still today, there is no consensus on the exact number that perished in this accident. On May 29, 2014, in Sainte-Luce-sur-Mer, the centenary of the catastrophe was observed. At 1:55 a.m., bells tolled in the churches of Rimouski and Sainte-Luce. Several descendants of the deceased were there, I hadn't paid attention, but doing research, I see that they spoke about it in the media. About thirty people took part in the commemorations and went to the sea, in the early hours of the morning, to where the sinking occurred.

Among the descendants of the victims, the great-grandsons of the commanders of the *Empress* and of the *Storstad*, the ship that threw the *Empress* into a scene of horror and chaos. They went just beyond the marine cemetery where lay the remains of some five hundred bodies, including several crew members. Among them, sailors barely twenty years old died that night, most of them from England, where the *Empress* was headed. Over there, on this same day in 2014, a mass was celebrated, attended by more than fifty families of the victims in a packed church.

Then the crowd moved toward the monument in memory of

those who lost their lives that night, and whose names were enumerated on the edge of the horizon until silence. The list of the deceased was read, the names uttered one by one, making the face of each one reappear, bringing back for some a flood of memories, and the engraved stone became an invisible ink illuminated by the fire of the words.

For a long time, this tragedy at sea was forgotten—although it was one of the most significant of the early twentieth century, with those of the *Titanic* and the *Lusitania*—probably because it occurred only two months before the outbreak of World War I, which rapidly overshadowed it.

Some people maintain that, out of the 2,200 passengers, 1,513 died. Others claim that the number of deceased was 1,491 out of 2,201 passengers. Elsewhere it's given as 1,057. The only number that doesn't change is that of the children. Out of the 138 children on board, five survived.

As if the fog refused to dissipate, the bodies become lost in the midst of the numbers undulating before our eyes, they merge into changing statistics that serve only to further confuse an already hazy image.

Among the clippings left in Simone's box, there is a page from a Quebec City newspaper listing the names of people whose corpses were removed and brought to the Rimouski wharf, transformed into a morgue for those days. The tragedy was unprecedented, no space in the city could receive so many dead, so a shed was set up in one spot where people arrived from everywhere to identify the demolished bodies, the faces of which were sometimes merely a vague impression in the eyes of their families.

Then there were the names of individuals whose remains were never found. In total, close to 1,500 people, on two large pages of the newspaper. We should read the list, Juliette tells me, to see if we know any. A friend is often the one who points out the blind spots that hide from us what we should look at, she immerses our head in a reality from which we would rather escape. Even though I dread the process, it's the only thing to do with this newspaper. In the middle of the left page, I believe I recognize two names.

Quebec City, 1958

FIRST THERE ARE TWO ROADS.
COITUS BRINGS THEM TOGETHER.
THEN THERE ARE THREE ROUTES.

They didn't expect a snowstorm in late April, when the ice cracks on the river, when people are putting away toques and scarves, and the high boots that made it through another winter.

The snow began to fall lightly. Then the winds rose, and only a swirl of white was visible.

Adrien doesn't let anything show, but he's nervous. Will the car start, I should have had the carburetor checked, he tells himself, I have enough gas, yes, I filled up the day before yesterday, but such a snowstorm in April I've never seen. It *would* have to happen this year...

He grabs the small suitcase, opens the front door, and immediately a cloud of snowflakes rushes into the hallway. I'll start the car, he shouts, it will have time to warm up before you're ready to leave! He takes a blanket.

He hopes it will be a boy, but he'll also be happy to have a girl, for a long time he's been wishing that Simone would get pregnant but it's nature that decides, and she's not really *keen on it*, he has to insist, at first he is tender, then he forces her to yield, a man needs to be satisfied, after all that's part of married life, he thinks. He unfolds the blanket and spreads it out over the back seat. Perhaps Simone would rather lie down than sit in front.

Nine months ago, he insisted. She remained unmoved when he approached to kiss her after an evening with plenty of wine among friends. A bit drunk, he embraced her more firmly than usual. Simone tried to free herself from his grip, but, dulled by alcohol, did not succeed, he grabbed her and pulled her toward the bed, ready to plunge into her, Adrien turned her around, face against the sheets, slammed his body up against hers, breathing heavily, murmuring inaudible words into Simone's ear, which his tongue explored with an assurance she hadn't known in him, then he brutally drove his sex into her, and doubtless she would have been frightened by this almost violent ardour had her body not been numb.

Stretched out on the bed, her face buried so deep in the pillow that breathing is difficult, Simone no longer really knows where she is, her body is so limp, she'd like another drink but can no longer move, Adrien lay down on her with all his weight, hurt her, but she doesn't have the courage to confront him, and he is so forceful tonight, she says to herself when she feels a stream of saliva run down into her ear, the smell disgusts her, she tells herself that if she tries, it would perhaps be enough to stop him, or she could shout, but the neighbours would hear and the situation would be terribly embarrassing, she gathers her strength and prepares to arch her back to give herself momentum, but then she feels a kind of tear in her belly and can no longer move.

Once sated, Adrien turned over to the opposite side of the bed and fell asleep thinking of a young woman he'd met three weeks earlier in Chicoutimi, in the bar at the hotel.

Kamouraska, 2018

HOW CAN GROWING OLD BECOME REBIRTH?

Our luggage ready, Juliette and I prepared to return to Montreal. She went to do the rounds of the Kamouraska art galleries before we left, while I went to walk again along the river. I wanted to look at it and hear it and breathe it in one more time before leaving. No doubt I hoped it would tell me another bit of the story.

The sky is grey, the expanse almost immobile, clouds shift in no apparent direction, wandering over waters that are still cold in this late April, the hours seem frozen like the colour of the water, the sand, and the rocks all around. The landscape is primarily an intimate contact with time, with the hundreds and thousands of years needed to shape the horizon that the light continues to recreate every day.

The images of my childhood are buzzing round, memories rush in, our winters in the mountains and our summers by the sea, Simone, a notebook in hand, so that's what she was writing then, her story, and poems brief and fragile as a butterfly's wing, like flickering lamps we light in the darkness of our lives, and that extend before us like a bridge until morning.

In these different-coloured notebooks—no pink, but blue for the days and years that unfold, and green and yellow for poetry—Simone copies out passages of poems and writes her own in the middle of pages like little buildings of words that manage to sustain the hours, lines that provide a balance, a constricted world that the poems expand. Simone records what makes possible a life torn between desire and love, the power of which continues to resonate, and the tensions of a couple wandering among the ruins.

Every morning she awakens to a mutilated existence she doesn't know how to inhabit, try as she may to extricate herself from the shell of her past to find again the missing part of herself, Simone only manages to wind up on a shore of crumbling shells and carcasses gnawed away at by time. She has ended up in a life that is not hers, in a marriage that is not hers, and her daughter knows nothing of the sinking of which she is perhaps the real survivor.

She writes poems and sometimes that's the only thing that manages to soothe her. She pulls her sorrow from the silence, lets the music of the words embrace her, then tells herself she'd like to go as far away as her poems.

How could I have forgotten it, this scene so often repeated in which Simone is seated, writing in a wide yellow notebook, the sound of her old ballpoint pen scratching the paper, her gaze wavers, going from the page to staring vacantly out past the sea, between the inexpressible and words, how could I have forgotten the times when, leaving school at the end of the day, I'd get into the car and my mother would immediately close the book she was reading, she'd smile and ask: *How was your day, Hanna?* Did I ever ask how her day went? Had Simone gotten toppled over or held steady on the quay of high winds, had she ventured into her forest pierced with poems, had she heard the birds of spring, seen some fireflies, or had the shadows continued to grow in her like pine trees shedding their needles?

I stop walking and sit on one of the rocks bared by the low tide. Simone joins me. She rests her head on my shoulder, tells me the birds have not closed their wings in our poems, the words keep the petals from creasing.

I am the little girl become the mother of my mother and of her unfathomable oceans, the little girl with the missing leg looking for the way home.

I see again Simone and Adrien, newlyweds on the shores of Lake Louise in the Rockies. My father often told me about their honeymoon, but it's another trip altogether that Simone describes in one of her blue notebooks.

The road was long, she writes. Scarcely arrived at the hotel, they went to stroll around the lake to stretch their legs. The landscape dazzled with its beauty—*cosmic beauty* is the expression Simone used. The glaciers form large curves that fall into emerald-blue waters. The day they arrive, the summits are covered in clouds, *The earth is beautiful* is the sentence Simone wrote, ending with these words: *but I cannot.*

Then she speaks of Eva's fiancé, the soldier whose name she doesn't know, but she knows she was going to marry him as soon as he returned from the front, he's the one she would have rather wed than Édouard, and the forest would have been a landscape of long shadowless stems. Had I been born of another father and in another life, Simone wonders, would I have loved Antoine, would I even have loved?

SOON WE WILL NOT DISTINGUISH
BETWEEN SHADOWS AND LIGHT

I get up to return to the hotel where I must join Juliette. I place Simone's boxes on the back seat of the car, pile the luggage in the trunk.

Once she is ready to leave again, Juliette suggests we continue down the river to Rimouski rather than return immediately to Montreal. Juliette had never heard of the tragedy of the *Empress of Ireland* before I told her about it. I myself was unaware of it all until I discovered the newspaper articles.

On the road that runs alongside the river, I speak to her of the Finnish immigrants who were returning to Europe, couples separated just when the ocean liner was sinking— sometimes one of the two survived, or perished trying to save the other—some drifted for two days on pieces of wood before being rescued. Death infiltrated their eyes and never left. Juliette remembers that I spoke to her of 133 children lost that night, swept away in scarcely a few minutes from their dreams that would remain forever unfulfilled.

But the newspaper articles, Juliette asks me, how was your mother able to find them? They date from 1914, Simone wasn't even born. Do you know why she was so interested in this sinking? I imagine it must be strange to realize you know nothing about your mother. In fact, I don't know mine either, she adds, I never even tried to piece together my story, or retrace it. I know so little about my adoptive parents, my father left for the factory every morning at five-thirty, already exhausted and disgusted by this life of misery handed down from father to son where people hurled orders at him in a language he didn't understand. As soon as he stepped through the door of the house at four o'clock, he'd go straight to the fridge and pour himself a first beer while my mother made dinner that he would view with distaste—she did nothing but take care of Juliette since they adopted the little girl who she'd overprotected to the point of smothering, her father told himself, Juliette had only been three months old, her mother couldn't raise her alone so it was us or the orphanage. Micheline wanted so much for them to take Juliette, I ended up agreeing to please her, but we died that day, or perhaps were already dead well before, it doesn't matter, it's too late now, he thought again, opening another beer at the moment that his wife quickly left her cooking to greet Juliette, who was returning from school.

From my childhood, Juliette continues, I remember nights when my mother took me into her bed with her, and when she'd hear the kitchen door open, she hurried to bring me back to my room.

She tucks me in and asks me to close my eyes, to imagine we are both at the seashore, that we are swimming or playing together, building a sandcastle that we offer up to the next tide. Then my mother leaves the room...

Juliette then hears shouting and blows, a door slamming, objects flung against the wall, she buries her head under the pillow—does she wonder at that instant why she ended up in this family?—the shouting is too loud, like every time, she's afraid he'll kill her mother, so she gets up and goes to the kitchen, where she sees her father's arm raised high in the air, then come down violently on the face of her mother, who is already crouching near the fridge. Her father turns to Juliette in tears, sends her back to her room, shouting that this is a matter for adults, but Juliette doesn't move, her gaze meets that of her mother, who doesn't let her out of her sight, the father knows he cannot touch his daughter, he could not cross that line, otherwise, he knows, his wife will kill him.

Do poems save us from the violence hiding away deep inside people? Juliette wonders. She knows that a poem has the strength to drive us brutally away from childhood. She has not forgotten the one she read at age fifteen, she could no longer bear that horizon obstructed by the past, had taken refuge at Hanna's for the night. In the morning, she knew that her childhood had come to a close.

A child is busy building a village
It's a town, a county
And who knows
   By and by the universe.

Painting, Juliette tells me, is perhaps my way of responding to this intimate violence, to consent to the movement of the shadows.

It's perhaps also what I do. Consent to the movement of shadows. Everything seems so clear for Juliette. She has always seen her path and followed it. Even if she doesn't know where she comes from and who her biological parents are, even if the sound of blows is her only legacy, and she grew up with a mother who enclosed her in the cage of her love, it's as if Juliette has always sensed she would escape, would no longer be of that world—as a little girl, does she already know that art could save her and that the studio of colours and papers will become her only home?

We don't know what makes it possible to illuminate the path toward oneself, Juliette continues. Do you remember our games, when we were children? Rather than playing with dolls or having tea, we imagined an art gallery where my drawings of gardens, mountains, and forests were exhibited. You welcomed our fictitious visitors to whom I explained at length the meaning of each of my works. After haggling over their price, they'd leave with a painting under their arm. With that money, we could then buy an apartment with several rooms where the two of us would live. We invented games that we wanted to resemble our future lives. Art had perhaps begun to save us.

Juliette knew quickly how to transform her world of silence and shouting into abstractions that renew our way of perceiving and feeling things. Personally, as soon as I began to write, I understood that the work on language brought out a host of uncertainties and fragilities, and that the words dug into the muffled uneasiness that hounded me.

Then one day they began to move differently on the page. Without talking about it to anyone, I wrote poems. Suddenly language seemed to me to seek shafts of light, yes, it was probably what I had wished for in secret, between my classes at the university, or in my room, the evenings when I wasn't with Juliette, I wrote to find *real life*, the one that was elsewhere, unaware that in the next room my mother was seeking the same thing.

I wanted to discover the origin of the shadow in the young woman that I was, eaten away at by sadness come from nowhere, that cast a veil over the horizon. I watched people live joyfully and love, but I was incapable of either. In the next room, Simone filled a yellow notebook.

Words, I sensed, would invent in me other paths than the one that appeared each morning as, powerless, I witnessed a rift I could not repair. By kneading them like clay, I recreated the meaning of things. Each poem I wrote pierced an opening in the darkness, breathed into the fog that hung over the house.

Juliette doesn't agree, but for me, identity needs truth. I have to know the sole survivor that I am of a troubled history, and be aware of the sinking from which my family did not escape.

Sainte-Luce-sur-Mer, 1914

THE HOUR OF COOL DRAFTS FROM
EXTINGUISHED STARS

Arthur Corrigan, his wife, Emma, and their four-year-old son line up on the quay. They are preparing to board the ocean liner that will bring them back to England to complete the formalities. Arthur decided to immigrate to America, more specifically to Canada, where he can easily find work and enjoy peaceful days. He knows that Europe is threatened by war and wants to shield his family. He is twenty-four, Emma twenty-three, nothing is yet set for them, they can build their life in this new land, far from world conflict. As he suffers from a slight handicap—a malformation in one leg—he'll be exempt from military service and won't go to the front if Canada joins the war that is brewing.

The little boy is agitated, he so liked the crossing to Canada that he's eager to reboard the boat! At the same time, he's impressed, a thousand times he asks his father, *How can it stay afloat, such a big ship, and if the winds get very strong and the waves very high, will it be knocked over?* Patiently, Arthur explains to his son how ships float and reminds him that the sailboat he takes his bath with has never capsized despite all his attempts!

The little boy adores the ocean. During the crossing, he urges his parents to take him to the deck to see the sun appear on the horizon, he believes it's a magic trick performed by the captain, in the evening, the kite must be put away, so all three return to the deck, to the opposite side of where they were in the morning, and watch the slow ending of the captain's magic trick.

That night, the stars went out.

Arthur and Emma did not return to England, did not come back to Canada, did not settle in Calgary, and Arthur was not hired by the Canadian Pacific Railway, he did not become one of the senior executives who decides the routes for new lines linking the country from west to east, did not return home at the end of his workday to find his Emma making dinner and their son studying to enroll in university the following year, he wants to be an engineer and also work for the company that contributes to building the greatness of this country, their new country.

That night, their lives were snatched in fourteen minutes by an opening of four by fourteen metres in the hull, while sixty thousand gallons of water entered the steamship operated by Canadian Pacific. That night, the stars went out above more than one thousand passengers on the *Empress of Ireland*.

Emma was sound asleep, she didn't hear the rumbling that foretold what happened next. Like so many others crammed into the uncomfortable third-class cabins, she was seasick. As soon as the boat lifted anchor, she drank some herbal tea to relieve the nausea gnawing away at her, seemingly innocuous herbs, but they caused her to feel such lethargy, surprising that she was so deeply asleep when the rumbling transformed into a deafening noise.

When she opens her eyes, she sees a few objects floating, doesn't know where she is, her husband's arm is reaching out toward her, but it moves away in a light mist that contrasts with Arthur's panicked face, this drowsiness, this slight drunkenness, feels so good she makes no effort to extend her arm and grab the hand of the man she loves, scarcely one second later she thinks of their son, their marvellous little four-year-old—where is my child, playing with his toys perhaps, Emma wonders before gently closing her eyes on her life.

Arthur saw Emma sink to the depths of the glacial waters, could do nothing for her, everything happened so quickly. After breaking down the door to their cabin, he took his son in his arms and pushed him into the corridor, which was not yet submerged. At the same moment, another door opened by the water pressure, and the little four-year-old boy turned around, he saw his father being thrown by the wave, then began to run.

Pointe-au-Père, 2018

THE VOICE OF HOPE, ABOVE THE DIN—
HOW CAN WE MAKE IT HEARD?

During the car trip from Kamouraska to Pointe-au-Père, Juliette wanted to know more about what I'd read in Simone's notebooks.

I told her about the real-life story with Antoine, that he was killed when a cargo ship collided with his sailboat, on the river, in May 1949, near Les Éboulements, that love remained raw like a wound never closed, like a breaker that threatens without ever crashing.

I didn't tell her that the green notebooks contained poems that Simone copied out, others that she wrote, and that it had been a shock to me to learn that my mother wrote poetry.

Juliette grabbed one of the notebooks from the box on the back seat and read one of the pages aloud.

I slept beneath the tree of silence
fastened to the branch that tears the horizon
only the sap from my wound
still flows.

I've been walking since your absence
I'm this coward separated from herself

who hides away beneath the rock
and if I awaken without a voice
I'll die again.

When she finished reading it, I told Juliette that I too wrote poems. *Yes, for a long time. No, I never had anyone read them.* She didn't seem surprised. She didn't ask me why I had hidden it from her. She simply said that she'd really like to read them one day, if I wanted.

Entering the *Empress of Ireland* Museum, which features exhibitions on the history and the sinking of the steamship, we headed to the room dedicated to the memory of the passengers.

THAT LITTLE PHRASE I DON'T KNOW—
IT'S SMALL, BUT IT FLIES ON MIGHTY WINGS

Was I driven by the desire to be loved by my father to the point of paying little attention to the bond I had with my mother? She loved me, I sensed it, and I wanted to believe that was enough for me. I had nothing to win, nothing to lose, whereas with my father everything was to win and I could lose everything—first his love, I thought. Or perhaps he seemed to be the more solid of the two, so I would stake everything on him.

I don't remember having confidence in Simone. Not that she was what they'd call *a bad mother*, but I couldn't manage to get her, to reach this woman, *my mother*. She seemed to me to walk on the other side of the shore.

The only opening from her world to mine was that of the constant dangers lying in wait for me, multiplying and nestling in every nook and cranny. Simone was ready to respond at the first sign of threat. For her, everything became a question of survival. I didn't doubt her love and she didn't speak of it, endeavouring to keep me under a bell jar. And at the end of the day her daughter, like her, survived.

It is night. I hear my mother's footsteps. I get up and go to the living room doorway. She remains motionless in front of a window overlooking the street. The whitish wisp at the end of the cigarette she holds in her hand makes all sorts of scribbling close to her face. This scene, repeated so many times. Often I am still awake when my father cautiously opens the front door and finds Simone in the living room. Her tears. Their shouting. My head beneath the pillow.

Can poems give us a life that we did not have?

I don't know who this woman is, did I even have a bond with her other than that of parent and child? *My mother. Her daughter.* Love is a given, then the time can slip by without adding anything.

Isn't that what happened in my first book? I spoke of my childhood, but Simone, it was pointed out to me, hardly exists in it. My father prepares the way in the universe before me, together we go to the tops of mountains, but my mother is absent from the journey.

She in her notebook, I in mine, did we hold the dialogue we didn't have, and would we end up talking to one another?

Is poetry our secret bond made of words never uttered, is it the reverse side of absence, a rain shower coming down to illuminate a nighttime garden?

I would like to have walked alongside my mother, for her to take my hand in hers and for me to feel the layer of time penetrate from one generation to another, from one woman to another, I would have relied on her life to build my own. But Simone is my distant mother and I am her alien daughter.

Today I hover round her like around my birth, I listen carefully to find out from what secret I was born, and what the missing piece is that cast shadows in every room in the house.

Les Éboulements, 1949

I WILL GO AWAY,
WITHOUT A DESTINATION

Antoine had cleaned his sailboat—the deck, the cabin, even the hull—she was immaculate. As he had the day before, as he would perhaps do the following day, after returning to port in the late morning, he'd worked on his boat for several hours, he'd donned clean clothes and made sure everything was impeccable on board before lifting anchor again.

He's scarcely carried out the manoeuvre when he sees his father's face appear, mouth open, eyes filled with fright, sees his mother's body and thinks he feels the warmth of her embrace when a harsh wind swells the sails of the *Beata*, carrying the broken memories of his childhood to the open sea.

Throughout the spring, Antoine would leave port at the end of the day, sail to the Lower St. Lawrence, and, after sunset, when the cold overtook the mildness of the day and the fog began to ripple like a ragged cloud above the water, he would drop anchor at random and go down to the cabin to lie on the berth he shares so often with Simone, that narrow bed filled with their embraces.

How to cross from purgatory to the promised paradise? Antoine wondered, picking up the book by Dante that remained open on the table. I cannot enter into this life with

Simone and remain the amputee who every day tells himself he shouldn't be there... If I turn around, I'll see her tiptoe over the years, smiling, she's carrying our children in her arms—am I this old man already dead by her side, this man who cares for nothing, wandering in the labyrinth of her steps? If I look ahead, I see only the cold water of the past that paralyzes me and faces disappeared in the silence of the river.

I escaped the final wave. But what worth has my existence that cost my father his life? What arms can repair the wrench of being torn from those of my mother? At the bottom of this river their bodies lie, without farewells and without burial, the night was without destination.

Only five of us survived... I should be grateful for those years given to me as a reprieve, content to have been adopted, surrounded by friends, and when I embrace Simone, I should be the happiest of men for not having drowned. But I cannot free myself from my father's grip just before he threw me into the corridor, snatched at the same instant by a wave that smashed down the door of the cabin next to ours.

I remember being frightened before boarding the steamship, we had done the crossing in the reverse direction, and it went well, but I was terrorized. I didn't want my father to know, so I feigned curiosity, asked him a thousand questions—how do boats float, Dad, and what if the waves become very high and the winds very strong...?

My parents, Arthur and Emma, lie at the bottom of these waters, Antoine tells himself again, forty-three metres deep, their hearts have stopped beating. And mine at the same time.

In the middle of the misty river, Antoine's sailboat turns slowly around on itself, like a blind prey, it turns as a ship approaches, nothing is visible in that fog, but a quiet and decisive impact can be heard, it is a cargo ship taking in its mouth a part of the sailboat's hull and crushing it.

Each evening I allow fate to decide the moment when I will rest with the drowned.

I was never able to warm up from that night, soon I will learn what boats do when waves too powerful swallow them. Simone will forgive me, when she discovers that the ship that will strike my sailboat is one I've called out to every night, for thirty-five years, so it can consume my already destroyed life, says Antoine, and

all of a sudden emptiness.
Hostile silence.
The knife of cruel surprise.
The gaping openness of eddying.
Insidious, inviting you to be engulfed,
and you do not refuse.

Pointe-au-Père, 2018

THE SUN ROSE HIGHER

In the room dedicated to the memories of passengers, Juliette and Hanna stopped in front of a large table reconstructing the connections between the victims of the sinking of the *Empress of Ireland* and the survivors who came forward to show their affiliation with those who perished in the tragedy.

A long shiver runs through Hanna when her eyes spot a name they think they recognize. She remembers a newspaper clipping found in Simone's box. The notice that appeared at Antoine's death stated he'd died in an unfortunate accident on the river on May 22, 1949, near Les Éboulements, Anthony Corrigan, the adopted son of Jules and Jeanne Tanguay.

Hanna stares at the board on which the names of the passengers and their descendants are written. She thinks she hears a choir of soloists chanting the words that washed up on this memorial, as if on a reef.

Peter Egan · Norman Carson · Dorothy Carson · John Allen · Phyllis Hogart · Elizabeth Hogart · Paul Beckett · Mary Beckett · Mark Baron · James Wilson · Gladys Wilson · Robert Abel · Rose Abel · (Tomas Abel) · Craig Quinn · Michael O'Neill · Alisson O'Neill · Tracy O'Neill · Joe Logan · William Maxwell · Margaret Maxwell · Tracy Maxwell · Dillon Marsh · Olivia Marsh · Jake Ford · Susan Ford · William Dunn · Sarah Dunn · Norman Austin · James Anderson · David O'Sullivan · Pat Bacon · Henry Lloyd · Dorothy Lloyd · Emma Milton · Abbie Milton · Peter Ryan · Jacob O'Brien · Iosep Ferris · Arthur Corrigan · Emma Corrigan · (Anthony Corrigan) · Gilbert Cunningham · Elatha Cunningham · David Quinn · Charles Wallace · George McCarthy · Dagan Tonner · (Brenda Tonner) · Art Tonner · Brian Ross · Fiona Ross · Brice McGivern · Luchar Gardner · (Tara Gardner) · (Kate Gardner) · Glenn Monaghan · Neal Williamson · Kiara Williamson · Trevor Jordan · Iollan Tormey · Tomas Shannon · Nolan McAlee · Roan Cowan · Etan Kells · Brenda Kells · Art Baker · Cormac Bannon · Abbie Bannon · David McVey · Charles Kelly · (Ailis Kelly) · Dagan Carmichael · Aslinn Carmichael · Dylan Tormey · Kate Tormey · Neil Cowan · Ross Greenfield · Luchar McCormack · Trevor Duffy · Sam Heaney · Roan McCartan

Kamouraska, 1949

FRAGILE IS SOMETHING THAT CAN BE BROKEN

Simone returned shivering from the river, tired out from her long swim. Every day she goes swimming like that, as far as she can, indifferent to the exhaustion that overcomes her when she faces the ebb of the waves.

After donning warm clothes, she goes back down to the living room to join her mother. Without a word, she sits down next to her on the couch. Two lives side by side, broken, advancing on the ruins.

Isn't there for each of us but one love, just one love that carries with it all the others, and in the end, only it will count? The others, if there were any, were just a way of wandering among the ashes of the castle destroyed by the tide.

And if, after finding love, after losing it, we look for it again, we'll be afraid of nothing. Not even of losing it. And failing to be able to experience this love, will we have missed everything? What if we retreat from it, out of fear of losing it? Simone's thoughts intermingle. Or maybe it is those of her mother, who suddenly asks her to make tea. She stands up and goes to the kitchen.

At the same time that Antoine drowned, that night, Simone sank into the cold waters of absence, leaving at the bottom of the river the breath we call *heart*. Like Eva, she lost the person who carried with him the entire universe. That name—*Antoine*—no longer exists except for Simone.

I will remain true to that love, she tells herself, the days will burn like ice, I will always remain true to that love...

And never will Simone give herself to another man, even married, even pregnant by him, she who believes in the power of words will name her daughter *Hanna* so that a bit of *the grace that will be able to save her* will flow in her, and so that God, if he still exists, supports her because she will not be able to, refusing to embrace the joy of a love born of her flesh, this daughter born of a rescue marriage, of a salvation that failed and left the victim to rot at the bottom of the water.

What will my life as a shipwreck victim be? Simone wonders, bringing a tray with two cups of tea to the living room.

Route 132 to Montreal, 2018

NOW YOU KNOW WHERE AND HOW
THESE LOVING SPIRITS WERE CREATED

Leaving the museum, Hanna and Juliette go walking alongside the river. They remain silent while the sun begins to close the horizon.

A few hours ago, Juliette thinks, Hanna was still Simone's mother, the one who wanted to repair her nights. Sometimes we think we know the most important things about people close to us. Sometimes we suffer, and this suffering was born long before us. Hanna was swept away by a current whose source she did not know, she slid gently between her father and her mother, while the years intensified the fog.

We have been friends forever, Hanna and I, this bond goes through time, she tells herself again. Without vows, without a contract or sacred ritual, without the obligations to which we are bound by blood ties, the friendship we have is probably one of the freest and most natural expressions of love. We are in one another's lives to share moments like this, connected by silence and beauty, by the stories we know and those we don't.

Barefoot in the cool sand, Hanna recalls stormy days at sea. When she was little, Simone would interrupt her games and take her to the big bed in her room. When they clung to one another like that, you couldn't tell who was afraid and who was reassured. Hanna loved those afternoons when she remained buried under the sheets, her back anchored against her mother's body.

Hanna now knows why, at the end of her life, Simone refused to return. She didn't want to travel again the road from Quebec City to Kamouraska, revisit those years, or walk alongside the river that had given her everything and taken everything away.

She guessed that one day her daughter would open the closet, discover the box filled with her memory, take hold of it with the others and place it on the ground, carefully cut the adhesive tape surrounding the cover, and lift it. There her story hid, scattered in fragments that Hanna would piece together, if she wanted.

Hanna could patch together the time, as Simone could have done when she was handed a letter Antoine had written to her shortly before beginning to lift anchor every morning to reach the open sea and hope not to return. But she never wanted to open it. Never wanted to know. As opposed to Simone, her daughter would perhaps want to know the entire story.

Hanna and Juliette returned to the car. I'll take the wheel, Juliette said. And they travelled on the 132 West, which was beautiful that day, the light raced over the river as they drove alongside it, they chose the slow route, the one of sailors who master the currents and, at one with the wind, await favourable tides.

My mother chose me, says Juliette, she confined me in the room of her love, whereas you depended on that of your father. It's true, Hanna replies, until now I belonged to my father, the man who gave me a love knotted with a thousand conditions. With him, I swam in oceans, climbed mountains, travelled in dreams and on road maps that he taught me to read. I had to meet his many great expectations. I don't ever remember having fun with my mother, my games didn't seem to interest her, she was there but elsewhere. I spent my adolescence in books, and since we didn't have any at home, I went to the library every Friday night, to borrow the ones I would read during the week. I don't remember my mother ever coming with me.

Nor did she ever speak to me of poetry, or read me her poems, not even those childish rhymes that teach you the names of trees and animals. Before going to school, I shared my days with her at home. Time passed, the years went by. Every day told me she was far away, there was a vacant, silent space inside her. She took care of her mother, her brother, her sisters, in addition to being entrenched in permanent tension with Adrien, and that filled the house, filled her life. She loved me, at least that's what I wanted to believe, she who tried to protect me from every imaginable danger. That's how she saw her role of mother. So I stopped waiting, stopped hoping that something other than that worried love could connect us.

I come from a mother who was not part of the family she had started. Perhaps she had let even her capacity to love drift. I belonged to my father, and Simone conveyed that to me every time the opportunity arose—go see your father, he'll take you, ask your father, he'll answer you... Adrien, take your daughter in your arms, she said to him, as if holding out a gift that she denied herself.

I come from a stranger in a life that was not her own. Adrien, she hoped, would save her from turmoil and offer her a world. She'd dreamt of a waveless sea stretching out to a smooth horizon, she found only a path of storms lined with sacrifices and humiliations in a marriage that drove her into total solitude as Adrien moved away from her. Powerless to keep his promise to shield her from suffering, he took advantage of his business trips to meet young women whom he imagined saving from a sad life in the seedy bars he regularly frequented.

Since childhood, Juliette and Hanna have shared what they experience and what they feel. The weight of family, but also the joys, demanding studies, broken romances, those that blossom, the choice of a life devoted to art. One knows of the other what she is sometimes unaware of in herself.

To words, Juliette always preferred oils and papers, glue, gouache, varnish, textures, and the light running across them. As opposed to words, she says, their violence cannot cause suffering. I like nothing more than to rummage in second-hand markets and unearth miscellaneous objects that seem useless and whose shapes don't call anything to mind, objects set down in the world just to be there.

Occasionally, Juliette brings back from her walks something she incorporates into one of the paintings she's working on. One day, on an engraving, she glued pieces of dead leaves from a plant gathered in a lane. She salvages everything. Her studio is a room of memories. Has the palette on which she mixes colours for the medium dried? She scrapes off that thick crust, crushes it, then applies it to the corner of a painting. And that is just the bit of colour that was missing.

Now that I've walked on the sand where my mother's life was lost, that I've been able to anchor my history in hers, Hanna says to her, I know that I belong to her. This emptiness I never was able to touch, never able to name, I see the source, it goes back to a river of generations, from my mother to my grandmother, and perhaps further still, the fear and sorrow of loss have entered me and begun to flow like blood from another body, from another heart connected to mine. Our lives resemble a forest where the visible trees are but a minuscule part—branches and trunks, leaves and buds—for, regardless of the species, beneath the earth there exists another world, and the trees are connected to one another by entangled roots, a hidden force that makes some perish and lets others survive.

I know now, Hanna adds, that each step redefines the path. No force can prevent us from loving. And no force can prevent us from dying.

I have loved several times, and each love stumbled, slamming up against a secret history whose weight I manage to grasp today. As if all joy were hindered, illegitimate, forbidden by a kind of loyalty from which I couldn't rid myself. Or I thought life was frozen in the blurry sensation of having lost something from the start.

Do poems lighten the part that weighs on us? Are they greater than reality, more powerful than love to transform it, or are they reality, are they love itself?

Kamouraska, 1951

SOME DAYS SETTLE SO THAT NOTHING CROSSES THE HORIZON

Morning entered the room by a thin shaft that passed through the garden. Soon it will skim over Simone's head, then run down the length of her neck, and at that moment she'll open her eyes, arise, and go to the window to admire the flowers. She'll imagine Antoine still asleep, nestled in the sheets.

She would have liked to awaken by his side every morning, to know, with unshakable certainty, that love triumphed over the night, every morning she would have liked to feel their desire enter her.

On the night table, Simone placed the envelope that Jeanne discreetly slipped into her hand during the funeral, after telling her she'd give her the newspaper clippings about Antoine. Jeanne had found that envelope in her room, clearly in view on the bureau, impossible not to notice it when she entered for the first time after the death of her son, the child who had been entrusted to them at age four as *a priceless flower*. She knew she could never repair her son's heart and that no love would be stronger than the last gaze of his father, Arthur, who at that moment called him *Anthony*.

Simone does not open the envelope. She feels Antoine's breath on her neck and on her chest, tells herself that the sea keeps intact the memory of the lives it has sunk.

Quebec City, 2018

TIME REBORN

On the road back, Hanna and Juliette stopped in Quebec City. Hanna wanted to see once again the red brick house where she was born and had lived during her childhood and adolescence. The street carries a name of the sun, and it is there, on the sunny side, that everything began for Hanna. She was happy for this sign that Juliette pointed out to her.

That was where she had taken her first steps and learned to talk, where she'd read and written her first words, where she'd heard Martin Luther King's speech on the television, seen the assassination of John F. Kennedy, then a man walked on the moon, and from that moment on, she understood that there were other dreams and stories, other countries, other planets. The world was vaster than the house where she lived.

In that red house her life had begun. Is it there that Hanna sensed that words said more than what she heard? Is it there, for the first time, that she wanted to care for them, to tear them from the silence and the shouting that mutilated them?

There were so many words that Hanna didn't understand, though they were among the simplest: *love, time, departure*, and even *house*, even *family*. There was another world, that of words, and it was perhaps in that room with the floral wallpaper, upstairs in the red house, that Hanna, for the first time, had an inkling, that she thought: I could write it, just as Juliette said to herself: I can make it exist, this other world, I'll transform it into paintings, and thereby be able to live in it.

I'll tell stories, for aren't they what we leave behind? Isn't that what remains of our lives, these stories of birth, love, and death that are their very fabric? I'll entrust to words this strange adventure so they can give it meaning, she thought. They'll keep it alive, beyond our footsteps that will be erased, the words will preserve the memory of it, and what has been lived before me I will give to what comes after me.

Each in her own way, Hanna and Juliette would ask everything from art, from poetry: that they open up a reality other than the one seeking to enclose them. But it was only later, long after leaving her room of flowers that had since wilted, after closing the door of the red house, that Hanna understood that writing does not repair rifts, it only opens the paths needed for us to reconcile with them.

Juliette's adolescence was spent accumulating relationships that broke off after three, four, or six months. At age twenty she met Frédéric, a forest ranger who introduced her to the joy of swimming naked in the middle of a lake, to the silence of mountains in winter. Eight years later, their paths separated. A little wind lifts and too much wind overturns. She learned it at that moment.

At fourteen, Hanna thought it impossible to reconcile all the worlds she saw opening up and make the multitude of beings that lived inside her coexist. The child of yesterday and the adult of tomorrow, sometimes the man and sometimes the woman, one day of the city and another day of the forests, on one side art and literature, on the other medicine and law, how to choose one sole path, one sole identity, she wondered then, and how to know who you are if you don't know from which story you are born?

Hanna looked at her mother, looked at her father, she was fourteen, seventeen, twenty years old, and told herself that love, a relationship, a family must be that, that continual struggle for survival, without ever giving in, but persisting toward an invisible light in which you must unfailingly believe so as to exist in this dark room. In the evening, she would look up toward the stars that didn't set and invent absolute love for herself.

At twenty-three years old, she married. The morning of the ceremony, her father asked her if it was just to leave home. She said no. To not hurt him. Two years later, she divorced. Then she was caught in the trap of passions that tore her apart like violent winds, romances without love, and even when love was there, a shadow inside her began to stir, blurred the transparency of that love, until it was no longer visible, and the storm swept across the horizon.

When she read her own story in her mother's words, Hanna felt that life had finally been given to her entirely, that a new intimacy was opening inside her, words carried by her true voice taking hold. She stopped being afraid of the void that arose from nowhere, impossible to name.

One day the wind speed increased, and everything that gradually disappeared over the years reappeared. Hanna couldn't make her mother happy, her presence erased nothing, she couldn't fill the absence of the person missing from every single day, with whom she had sunk one night in the spring of 1949, as he himself had slid into darkness with his father and mother one night in the spring of 1914. From one life to another, there is no end. We unravel, we repair what we can.

Hanna closes her eyes. She no longer sees the red house and the garden of the child that she was, but a blue ocean, and from the bottom of this ocean, she begins to rise to the surface. She thinks she recognizes Tintoretto's *Paradise*, the painting that so impressed her when she saw it in Venice, as she slowly rises to the surface of her life.

WRITING ABOVE RIVERS

The clouds begin to break. Hanna now holds in her hands the story that separated her from Simone. She sees the man of the days and the man of the nights in her mother's heart, the shadows that, blindly, went back up the river and devoured it like a spring tide. Her love for Antoine ran through her entire existence, intact, like a wave that finds no shore, no rock to curb it. Above the red brick house, fragments of blue cut a path.

Through silence and blood, poetry entered Hanna's eyes and mouth, she can now spit out the storms that crushed the childhood home, prevented her life from taking shelter beneath her mother's gaze, from developing, sheltered from her father's wishes.

How many days do we live?

Above all, how many days go by without our being numbed by the years, dulled by a series of footsteps without dreams? Where does this human journey buffeted by storms go? Can we keep alive the world that dwells inside us through the people who preceded us? Or with time do we become merely the survivors of a multitude of shipwrecks?

It would seem that the more we age, the more the answers escape us. Perhaps they also matter to us less. We are walking in a forest where most of the trees rise to the sky, where some lean against others to regain their strength, some are already dead, there were nights so dark we no longer knew how to move forward, there were light mists, ice storms, there were seasons, dreams and torments, loves and friendship broken, sometimes found again.

Above all, there was this brightness between the trees. We learned to see this path, to follow it too. Wherever we are, a stream reaches the river where the present runs, a river and an ocean will end up carrying away our absent ones they let time and our stories flow past. The poem is perhaps the tenuous and precious moment when thin ice forms at the surface of a waterway that too strong a ray could tear,

> like a flame that bows and leaps,
> as sound waves pass,
> poignant as first love remembered,
> the past, the lost, the never-to-be
> glimpsed between the coming and the gone.

When Hanna returns to the car where Juliet waits for her, she knows she has extricated herself from her former shell, that she's now found what was missing to allow her to enter a new dwelling. She will not be merely the survivor of a love that ran through her mother's life all the way to the end.

Above the red brick house, the sky has brightened. Birds begin to fly.

Hanna opens the rear door of the car, lifts up the box cover, and removes the sealed envelope containing Antoine's letter. She sits down on the seat, carefully tears the seal, and removes the sheet of paper wrinkled by time.

She reads the words that describe the slow descent into

despair. Antoine speaks of the rift he has felt since he was four. He describes the suffering he feels awakening each morning with his father's gaze penetrating his, then the hours that follow, feeling like a stranger in this life that should not even have been, and to which nothing can give meaning.

Hanna reads the words of Antoine, who cannot bear the sight of Simone's rounding belly, he cannot imagine becoming a father in turn, his gaze penetrating that of this child to whom the woman he loves will give birth three months later, a child who will have the blood of a survivor who sank, he too, one night in May 1914.

Hanna reads these words that her mother could not bring herself to read.

A wave forms in the distance. From what mist does it emerge, and how high will it rise when it reaches the shore where Simone walks toward her daughter, watching her tear off another of the veils that connect them? Hanna thus receives, intact, the secret that, like an unmoored buoy, has risen to her from the murky water of the river.

Simone takes her daughter's hand. Together they move toward the open sea. Their grief overhangs the river, no longer knows where the waves come from or where the light goes. Absence has changed into an expanse of blue to never again close.

AUTHOR'S NOTE

For the passages concerning the *Empress of Ireland,* I consulted various sources, including sites dedicated to that tragedy.

The title of this novel comes from a poem by Yves Bonnefoy, and some titles of chapters are quotations:

To live means following the traces of the child that you were, Marc Alexandre Oho Bambe

Going home (there where you describe your chase, your journey, your harvest, your origins), Pascal Quignard, trans. James Kirkup

The world of childhood is a hanging gondola waiting for something to arrive, Anne Dufourmantelle

There is the light that falls, Eugénio de Andrade

You plant your world somewhere, elsewhere or not, Silvia Baron Supervielle

A breath of water in the dark, Anne Hébert

The rim of the heart is cloudy, Chen Yuhong

The shadows had already fallen, Carlos Drummond de Andrade

Nothing can be understood without interlacing, Richard Texier

The half-finished heaven, Tomas Tranströmer

At the end of my suffering there was a door, Louise Glück

You never completely learn to be out of your depth, Chantal Thomas

I left to dive into the black hole of living, Marc Alexandre Oho Bambe

And I saw the close of day and the falling tree, Gabrielle Wittkop

Like the cloud chooses the landscape, Carlos Drummond de Andrade

Darkness had time to fall, Tomas Tranströmer

There was a little more light in the water, William Faulkner

First there are two roads. Coitus brings them together. Then there are three routes.
  Pascal Quignard
How can growing old become rebirth? Yves Bonnefoy, trans. Hoyt Rogers
The hour of cool drafts from extinguished stars, Wisława Szymborska, trans.
  Stanisław Barańczak and Clare Cavanagh
The voice of hope, above the din—how can we make it heard? Yves Bonnefoy,
  trans. Hoyt Rogers
That little phrase "I don't know" [...] It's small, but it flies on mighty wings,
  Wisława Szymborska, trans. Stanisław Barańczak and Clare Cavanagh
As I go away, without a destination, Carlos Drummond de Andrade
The sun rose higher, Virginia Woolf
Fragile is something that can be broken, Émile Littré
Now you know where and how these loving spirits were created, Dante, trans.
  Allen Mandelbaum
Your own life is your truest story, Jim Harrison
Some days settle so that nothing crosses the horizon, Ann Lauterbach
Time reborn, Pascal Quignard

Excerpts of poems by Rainer Maria Rilke, trans. Susanne Petermann (p. 13); Charles Baudelaire, trans. Richard Howard (p. 14); Dante, trans. Allen Mandelbaum (p. 63); Hector de Saint-Denys Garneau, trans. John Glassco (p. 104); Olga Votsi (p. 125); and Kathleen Raine (p. 154) are found in this novel.

Musical works accompanied me as I wrote and reread my novel, embodying in a sense the rhythms, chords, and tone of the writing.

To share them, I've grouped these works in a playlist you can find on Spotify by searching for *Pas même le bruit d'un fleuve* or *Hélène Dorion*.

This music includes:

Max Richter ("On the Nature of Daylight," *The Blue Notebooks*, "Dream 1," "Mrs Dalloway: In the Garden") ·

Rauelsson ("Fluvial," "Wave In," "She/Swimming," "Messy Hearts") ·

Ólafur Arnalds ("Reminiscence," "Verses," "Þú Ert Jörðin," "Only The Winds") ·

Jóhann Jóhannsson ("Flight from the City," "The Drowned World," "A Deal with Chaos") ·

Nils Frahm ("Immerse!," "Four Hands," "Went Missing," "Doria— Island Songs VII," "All Armed)" ·

Armand Amar ("Save Us") ·

Yansimalar ("Areş") ·

Henryk Górecki (*Symphony No. 3*) ·

Pēteris Vasks (*String Quartet No. 4: V. Meditation*) ·

Philip Glass ("The Poet Acts," "Metamorphosis Two," *String Quartet No. 3: Mishima*) ·

Sigur Rós (*Ágætis byrjun*) ·

Esmerine ("The Space in Between") ·

Oiseaux-Tempête ("Notes from the Mediterranean Sea," "Bab Sharqi," "Aslan Sütü [Santé, Vieux-Monde!]") ·

Godspeed You! Black Emperor ("Storm") ·

Laurie Anderson ("The Water Rises," "Our Street Is a Black River," "Gongs and Bells Sing")

ACKNOWLEDGEMENTS

Thanks to Éditions Alto, publishers of the original edition of this novel, and to Book*hug Press for giving it a new life.

Special thanks to Jonathan Kaplansky, translator and friend, for all the care he took in translating my novel, and for our stimulating exchanges.

All my gratitude to those close to me, who accompany me on this writing path and whose presence leaves so many traces in my books.

ABOUT THE AUTHOR

HÉLÈNE DORION is the author of more than thirty books, including works of poetry, fiction, and nonfiction. She has won many awards, including a Governor General's Literary Award. She is a recipient of the prestigious le prix Athanase-David, awarded by the Quebec government for her body of work and contributions to Quebec literature. A multidisciplinary artist, Dorion regularly exhibits her photographs and presents literary concerts with renowned orchestras. Her poetry collection *Mes forêts* is the first work by a living woman and a Quebecer to be added to the curriculum for France's baccalauréat. Born in Quebec City, Dorion divides her time between Orford and Montreal.

PHOTO: MAXYME G. DELISLE

ABOUT THE TRANSLATOR

JONATHAN KAPLANSKY won a French Voices Award to translate Nobel Prize–winning author Annie Ernaux's *La vie extérieure* (*Things Seen*). His translation of *Frank Borzage: The Life and Films of a Hollywood Romantic* by Hervé Dumont was a finalist for the Wall Award from the Theatre Library Association. Recent translations include Jonathan Bécotte's *Like a Hurricane*, Hélène Rioux's *The End of the World Is Elsewhere*, and the libretto of an opera by Hélène Dorion and Marie-Claire Blais entitled *Yourcenar: An Island of Passions*. He has also translated Dorion's *Days of Sand*. Born in Saint John, New Brunswick, Kaplansky now lives in Montreal.

PHOTO: VÉRO BONCOMPAGNI

COLOPHON

Manufactured as the first English edition of
Not Even the Sound of a River
in the fall of 2024 by Book*hug Press

Copy-edited by Stuart Ross
Proofread by Laurie Siblock
Type + design by Malcolm Sutton

Printed in Canada

bookhugpress.ca